THE ZEE BROTHERS: ZOMBIE EXTERMINATORS VOL.2

ZOMBIE SCHOOL LOCKDOWN

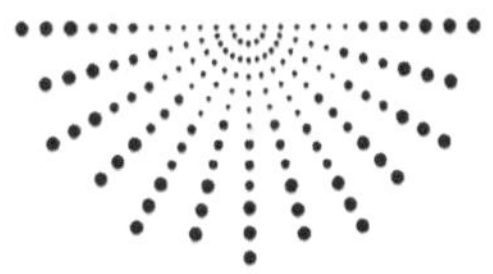

GRIVANTE

Edited by
KATY LIGHT

GRIVANTE PRESS

CONTENTS

To all you Zee Brother's fans,
We're glad you're back for more!

INTRODUCTION

Welcome to The Zee Brothers: Zombie Exterminators

If you are joining us for the first time, there are only a few things you need to know in order to enjoy this tale.

Jonah is a dominating, gruff, classical music loving badass, that calls the shots and keeps them coming.

Judas is a tobacco chewing, gun slinging, rock music loving goofball, that is a little slow to learn, but always has his big brother's back.

Together, they are The Zee Brothers: Zombie Exterminators.

In their last adventure, they met the woman of their dreams, hot and sassy JJ, along with her magical dog, Xanadu. Her dog has both the mysterious ability to slow time, in a weird disco music filled interlude sort of way and the uncanny ability to poop diamonds.

With their new friends help, the brothers put to rest an ancient curse that threatened to spark the zombie apocalypse, this all took place in The Zee Brothers: Curse of the Zombie Omelet. You can find it here!

While they survived mostly unscathed, their beloved truck, Sasha, was totalled during their escape attempt and their client, Larry, was dead before they even arrived. Feeling guilty about it and since Larry had no teeth with which to infect anyone, they brought their deceased client home with them.

Zombie School Lockdown takes place, approximately two weeks after Curse of the Zombie Omelet.

PART I - TOMBIE

THE DOOR to the office swung open as Bobbie sat a sign on the counter that read 'PTA Meeting', with an arrow pointing down the hall to the conference room.

Little Tommy Tucker walked in, his face pale, holding his hands across his stomach.

"Uhh," Tommy groaned. "I don't feel so good."

"Oh, I'm sorry Tommy. You do look a little green. Did you have too many Energy-Os this morning?"

"Uh uh." He shook his head.

She swung open the half door next to her desk that separated the office from the waiting area. "Come, lay down in the nurse's office. I'll call her to come check on you in a bit." She escorted him to the tiny room they called the nurse's office at Savini Charter School. It was a small room with a cot, a toilet, a sink and, thankfully, a tile floor, because as soon as little Tommy crossed the threshold from the carpeted office, he vomited.

Splash!

A gush of green chunky liquid poured out of the small boy. The spew splattered into a puddle that spread across the tile before them. Floating in the green ooze were red and black chunks. A stench of decay drifted up on little tendrils of steam and clung in Bobbie's nostrils.

She grabbed her nose as she looked at the floor and discovered that her white tennis shoes were firmly in the puddle.

"Ugg," she groaned, stepping back. *At least it didn't get on my new nylons.*

Tommy looked up with wide, tear swollen eyes. "I'm sorry," he whispered.

"Oh," Bobbie's heart broke. She patted his shoulder with her free hand. "We'll get this cleaned up and get you better. Go lie on the cot and I'll call the cafeteria to see if Nurse Janet can come check on you."

At her desk, Bobbie picked up the phone and buzzed the cafeteria. As she waited, Principal Hotchkins, a tall thin man with balding blond hair walked in. They smiled at each other.

"How long until the meeting with the PTA members?"

"About twenty minutes, a few of them are back in the conference room already." She scribbled Tommy's name in the sick log on her desk.

"Ok, I'd like to see you in my office beforehand. I need to relieve this stress." He smirked at her and adjusted his 'naughty stick' in his pants.

Of course you do. Just like every Monday.

"I'm trying to get Janet on the phone, Tommy Tucker is sick and I've got to clean—" an answer on the other end of the phone drew her attention away.

Principal Hotchkins broke his gaze from her chest when he caught wind of the odor, glanced toward the nurse's office and crinkled his nose. He made an ick face at Bobbie, pointed at his watch and then his crotch, then turned and disappeared into his office, closing the door.

Exactly what I was thinking. She shook her head and turned her attention back to the phone where Janet was speaking.

"I'm up to my arms in hamburger here, I've already got enough to do. Can't this wait?"

Bobbie took a deep breath and held the phone away from her ear a second. "Janet, we have a sick boy down here. Little Tommy Tucker, just threw up in the nurse's office. He's very green and doesn't look well."

After a moment of silence, Janet's voice returned, softer this time. "Alright, alright. Let me get this hamburger mixed and then I'll wash and head down. Give him something to put him to sleep, and I ain't got time to clean up his puke. I've got to get this hamburger cooking or none of the kids are getting lunch today."

"I know, Janet. I'll go check on him and get the floor scrubbed."

She slipped her soiled shoes off her stockinged feet and walked to the supply closet for cleaning supplies.

⚡

THIS IS SO GROSS.

Bobbie twisted the dark stained rag out into the bucket she'd filled with soapy water. She'd cleaned some nasty messes before, but this one was the worst. There were fleshy-feeling black chunks and red spots that were almost surely blood floating in the water. She refused to look too close at them. She'd been holding her breath the entire time; the stench made her stomach roll.

Tommy moaned on the cot and, after washing her hands, she opened the medicine cabinet and found 'the pills' they sometimes gave to sick kids that helped them sleep it off. She filled a small glass with water and sat on the edge of the cot.

"Tommy. Sit up, Tommy. I've got some medicine for you."

His eyes fluttered open, then closed again. His hands lay on his stomach, clutching open and closed. "It hurts," he whimpered. His cheeks sunken and his skin even more ashen and green now.

Bobbie reached behind him and lifted him up, her heart aching for the boy. "Here Tommy, take this." She scooted forward, the side of her skirt pulling up, exposing her thigh as she did so, and pushed the clear capsule through his pale lips. "Take a drink, swallow it down." She offered the water. "Later, you'll wake up and be all better."

She smiled at him as he sipped the water.

"Miss Jackson?" Principal Hotchkins' voice sounded behind her.

She jumped and turned.

The principal looked at the exposed tops of her stockings, then tilted his head to examine the boy. His face grimaced with concern and then he waved her over.

"How is he?"

"Not good."

"Nurse Janet on her way?"

"Yes, as soon as she gets cleaned up."

"Ok. Tuck him in and then come to my office. We'll call his parents."

"Yes, sir." She turned back to Tommy, but stopped when Principal Hotchkins grabbed her arm. She looked up into his eyes, which leered down at her chest.

"Thanks for the peek."

"What?" her forehead scrunched together.

His gaze shifted to her legs and he nodded at her skirt which had pulled up like a dance club mini, leaving her exposed all the way to her panties.

She blushed and tugged it lower.

He let her go and smiled. "Hurry up."

Bobbie walked back over to Tommy, who sat up with the cup of water in his hands, staring blankly ahead. She sat beside him, took the cup and set it on the floor. "It'll be okay, Tommy." She offered him reassurance while wondering when Nurse Janet would arrive. This was way over her head.

Tommy slumped forward groaning, she wrapped her arms around him, pulling him against her shoulder. "It's okay, Tommy.

Let the medicine kick in."

Please don't throw up on me. She squinted her eyes shut as she hugged him, reaching back to move her long blonde hair out of the way in case he got sick. Clothes were much easier to deal with than hair in that scenario.

She could feel him moving his mouth back and forth against her blouse near her neck line. *Is he trying to suckle? Poor kid. He needs comfort, but that's a little much.*

She was ready to break the hug when he bit her.

"Ow!" she cried out and pushed Tommy away.

"Tommy, why did you do that?"

Tommy let out a low moan and slumped against the pillow.

Bobbie stood and glowered at him. *Ow!* She rubbed the spot he'd bitten and noticed droplets of blood on her finger tips.

"Fuck!" The bite mark was red and swelling. She walked toward the door and looked back at Tommy. The sleeping pill appeared to have kicked in, he hadn't moved from the pillow. Either way, she decided to close the door behind her as she left.

She walked back into the office, pulling some facial tissue from a box, and dabbed at the blood on her skin, before heading to the principal's office.

Principal Hotchkins watched Bobbie walk around the corner, rubbing her shoulder. He stood and walked out to the reception area. "Are you okay? What happened?"

"He bit me!"

"What?" His eyes narrowed and he looked closer.

"I was trying to comfort him and he bit me. Something's really wrong with him."

"Ok, ok." He put his arms around her and turned her toward the open door of his office. "Here, let me help you. We'll call his parents and then see what we can do to take your mind off it." He closed the door behind them.

A moment later, the front office door swung open, and a third grader named Wendy wearing blonde pigtails came into the office.

"Hello?" the little girl said, sniffing the snot that threatened to drip out of her nostrils. "Is anyone here?"

Hearing no response, she pushed through the half door and wandered back to the nurse's office. The handle was hard for her to turn, but she twisted with all her might and pushed it open. Inside, she saw the small form resting on the cot. She walked closer until she realized that she recognized the boy.

"Tommy? Are you ok?"

PRINCIPAL HOTCHKINS PULLED a chair from the front of his desk around to the side and sat Bobbie in it. Sitting in his own, he looked her over and then reached for his phone with one hand as he typed Tommy's name into the computer with his other.

After a moment, his face twitched and he waited. "Mr. and Mrs. Tucker, this is Principal Hotchkins; your son Tommy is in the nurse's office. He's not feeling too well and we're gonna need someone to come pick him up. Please give the office a call back and let us know when you'll be here."

"There." He set the phone down. "That should do it."

Bobbie leaned forward in the chair he'd placed her in and stared at the floor. Her body felt stiff, her head ached and the bite on her shoulder burned.

Principal Hotchkins leaned in, smiling, and tried to catch her eye.

"C'mon Bobbie." He reached over, taking her hand and tugging her forward.

She looked up to the side, not meeting his gaze. "I don't feel so good, Hank."

He smiled and turned her face toward his. "It's okay. I'll make you feel better in a minute." He pulled her out of the chair and onto her knees on the floor before him, placing her hands on the zipper of his crotch. "C'mon now, you know what to do."

"But Hank..."

"Do it," he barked.

JANET MITCHELL, school nurse and cafeteria worker extraordinaire, pulled her hands from the mix of pink slime cafeteria meat and turned around to find a small blond girl with pigtails staring at her.

"I need a bang-bang."

"What?"

"For my boo-boo!" She held up her finger, which was red and swollen, blood dripping from a deep hole near the tip, the telltale signs of teeth marks around it.

"What happened?" Nurse Janet asked.

"I started sneezing." The girl stopped, sniffed, saying nothing more.

Janet waited a moment, then asked, "Well, what happened to your finger?"

"Oh," she said. "My teacher told me to go to the office and see the nurse. When I went in, no one was in the office. I walked down the hall and into the nurse's room. Tommy was in there sleeping. I sat on the cot next to him and saw his lips were red. I touched them and he bit me." She held her finger up again.

Janet's eyes grew wide, her body stiffening. "Tommy bit you?"

"Yeah. He's a big meany pants. I pulled my finger out and told him so and he just went back to sleep. I tried to reach the first aid kit, but it's too high for me. I came out into the office and heard Principal Hotchkins yelling at Bobbie in his office, it was scary, so I thought I might have better luck finding you in here."

Janet stared at the red and swollen finger, a knot tightening in her stomach.

"Ok, what's your name again?"

"My name's Wendy. Can I get a bang-bang for my boo-boo now?"

Janet shook her head and put on her best fake smile. "Sure thing, honey. I'll get you a bang-bang." She washed her hands and walked over to a first aid cabinet mounted on the wall and opened it, her mind racing. *Lunch starts in less than two hours. I need something to feed these kids. What am I supposed to do?*

Wendy watched as Nurse Janet peeled the covers off the sticky part of the bandage and rolled it onto her finger. "My mom always kisses it," she said expectantly.

"I'm sorry honey, I'm not your mom. They don't let us kiss boo-boos at school." She watched as tears welled up in the girl's eyes and sighed. "Here, honey." She bent at the waist and put her lips to the top of the bandage. "There, all better?"

Wendy beamed. "Thank you. My finger's better, but now my tummy hurts. And I know you're not my mom, but you do kinda remind me of my gramms."

Nurse Janet took Wendy's unbandaged hand and straightened one of the child's pigtails. "C'mon, let's get you to the office and see..."

NURSE JANET HUSTLED into the office with Wendy in tow, only to find it empty. No one was attending to the front desk and Principal Hotchkins's door stood closed. She shook her head. *Time for his 'Monday Morning Knob Job.'* She walked over and listened at the door.

"Uhh, uhh, that's right, take it!"

She grimaced and stormed down the hall toward the nurse's office. The bucket sat outside the door. "Surprised he let her get that done first," she spat. The stench caught her nostrils and brought her up short. Something inside her old bones twitched with familiarity. She looked through the small window to where

Tommy lay facing the wall, chest rising and falling, apparently asleep.

She spun Wendy around and opened the door across the hall. The testing room was dark and cool. Janet flipped on a light and spied the big office chair sitting before the computer desk and smiled. *Perfect!* "Come here, Wendy. See that big chair?"

"Yeah."

"Go sit down and make yourself comfy, I'm gonna check on Tommy and afterward I'll get Bobbie to write you a note so you can return to class. Ok?"

"Ok. Thank you."

Wendy climbed up into the chair, made herself comfortable and watched as Janet closed the door.

Janet took a deep breath, turned and opened the door to the nurse's office, whispering, "Tommy, are you awake?"

He didn't move. She stepped in closer, ignoring the foul odor, and peered over his shoulder. He had sunken cheeks and a ash-green pallor. She put her hand on his back; it was sweaty, yet chilled. She pulled him up and looked closer at his face. There was little color except the red on his lips that looked like... blood.

A long buried yet familiar feeling came over her from her days training to be a nurse for the Army. She gasped, stood and made for the door. Nurse Janet stopped short and turned back to the boy. *How? How could this be happening here?*

She closed the door behind her, clicking the lock and made her way to Bobbie's desk, where she pulled out the 'Emergency Services' binder and flipped through it until she came to the card she was looking for.

"Rogers Roto-Rooter,"

"Pests B' Gone,"

"Biohazard Bob's Clean-Up Service,"

"Emerson's Cooling & Heating,"

"Aha, that's the one!"

Zee Brothers: Zombie Exterminators
Jonah & Judas : Owner Operators
888-867-5309
Ask for Jenny
"We keep the dead, dead!"

PART II - THE ZEE BROTHERS

RING!

The side door to the garage the Zee brothers called home swung open. JJ Hembrook, wearing a tight pair of low rise blue jeans and a white tank top that had the faded words 'Suite Peas' stenciled across the chest, stepped inside. Her dog, Xanadu, close on her heels.

"Hello?" she looked around.

Judas lay sleeping on the couch, next to a coffee table littered with beer cans. One leg was on the floor, next to a few more empty cans. His bedroom door stood closed and a piece of paper with the word 'Larry' scribbled across it hung above it. Jonah's door was also shut.

Ring!

She chuckled to herself as Judas groaned. "I'll get it!" she called out and walked toward the kitchen. Xanadu wandered over to the couch and sniffed at the cans on the floor.

Jonah's beaten and battered flip phone lay plugged in, next to a pile of paperwork being held down by the 8-ball shifter. They had salvaged it from the remains of their truck, Sasha. The papers sat on the table he used for a desk near the window in the kitchen. The phone rang again and she snatched it up.

"Zee Brothers," she answered.

"Yes, hello. Is this Jenny?" a shaky female voice asked.

Smiling, then shaking her head, remembering the brothers' long running joke on their business card, she said, "Well, yes it is. How can I help you?"

"I need to report a possible outbreak."

"Are you safe?"

"Yes, I think so." The woman took in a deep breath.

"Ok, what's your name and where are you located?" JJ looked around for something to write on, but saw nothing useable except the paperwork in front of her. She moved the 8-ball aside, saw the title, 'Incident Report' and looked around for anything else she could possibly use. Jonah was still filling out these forms from the outbreak at Winter Oaks a few weeks back.

"My name's Janet, I'm the lunch lady and school nurse over at Savini Charter School."

JJ grabbed a pen and flipped the paperwork over. Scribbling on the back, she wrote the word's 'Savini School' "Ok, what is the situation there?"

"We've got a sick kid here, only," Janet's voice got quieter, "I've seen this before. The sunken skin, the green-grey pallor. I think he might be turning into a zombie."

JJ kept scribbling. "What do you mean, you've seen this before?"

"Well, I used to be a field nurse, back before the military was folded into the U.C.A., and I was on-site during the first chemically caused outbreak back in the sixties."

"Is he the only one? Where is he now?"

"He's asleep in the nurse's office, we gave him some sleeping pills and there is one other. A girl. She... well, he bit her."

A bell rang inside the school, the mid-morning bell, causing Janet to glance up at the clock, her hands gripping the phone tighter. Lunch needed to be in the oven cooking in five minutes or else they'd only be getting potato salad on their trays today.

"There's two?"

"Well, Tommy looks pretty green, the other one is just bleeding from her finger." A moan of pleasure came from Principal Hotchkins's office, causing Nurse Janet to scowl. She barked into the phone. "Look, what do I need to do? I've got two jobs to do and the only other job that's getting done around here is a blow job!"

JJ held the phone away from her ear a moment and looked at it, startled. "Ma'am if you can just keep an eye on them and don't let them out. I'll get the," she glanced at Judas snoring on the couch and then to Jonah's door which was still closed, "Um, the brothers over there right away."

"Look, I've got them in closed rooms. I'll let the principal know you're on your way. I've got to get back to the kitchen."

"Ok, ok." JJ said and then breathed a sigh of relief as Jonah's door swung open. She grinned as she took in the sight of him.

He walked out in nothing but a pair of boxers, rubbing his eyes. Seeing JJ standing in the kitchen, he smiled and squinted at the bright light coming in the window. He walked over, put his left hand on her back and looked down at her notes as she closed his phone.

"A school?"

"Yeah, she said she used to be an army nurse and had been present at the first chemically caused outbreak. She said it looked familiar."

"How many?"

"Two. A sick kid who looked like he was turning and another who he may have bitten."

Jonah shook his head. "Kids, that's never good. Ok. I'll get Judas and load up Sasha—, crap!"

They both looked out the window to where the demolished body of the brothers' modified 1950s Chevy pickup truck lay in pieces. Another leftover mess from their time at Winter Oaks.

"Can we take your Charger?" Jonah asked JJ, picking up the 8-ball and shaking it. It displayed the answer, 'Don't count on it'.

"Sorry sugar, I've got to take Xanadu to the groomers this morning. You're gonna have to take the rental the insurance company gave you until Dave's Custom Remodels can come and get Sasha and fix her up."

He looked at the red Prius parked next to JJ's Charger, lowered his head and sighed. "I'll go wake Judas."

"Hey, did you get my text?" JJ shuffled her feet.

"Huh?"

"My text message? I sent you a message last night."

"Oh," Jonah picked up his phone, flipped it open and fumbled around with the numerical keyboard. "I'm not really sure how—"

"XANADU!" JJ shouted.

Jonah's head swung around.

Judas shot up on the couch, the Arizona Diamondbacks baseball hat he always wore falling off, and looked around. "JJ?" he squinted.

"Dog nammit!" JJ stormed across the living area to where Xanadu had knocked over a half drunk beer and was lapping it up.

Xanadu looked up at her, licked the foam from his whiskers and waited expectantly.

Judas looked at Xanadu and then at JJ. "Where's all the disco and stuff?"

"That only seems to happen when he's in the air. I don't know how it all works." JJ picked up Xanadu and scolded him. "Beer is not for dogs!"

Jonah walked up behind her, "C'mon Judas, time to get up. We've got a job."

JJ tapped Xanadu on the head and walked over to the door with the hand written sign reading, 'Larry'. "May I?" She looked at Jonah with a raised eyebrow.

He bit his lip a moment then nodded.

She swung the door open and caught her breath.

Hanging from the center of the room, suspended from various ropes tied to eye-bolts in the ceiling and walls, Larry the Zombie stared at her. The ropes wrapped around his body in an ornate criss-cross harness, with intricate knots that held him immobile. The room smelled of daisies.

JJ turned to Jonah with a huge smile. "I see you've been practicing your rope skills!"

Jonah cleared his throat. "He makes a good rope bunny."

JJ giggled. "I'll be your rope bunny!" She made a little hop in his direction.

Jonah blushed and smiled back. "I'd like that."

Judas shot up from the couch. "We'd better get moving, Jonah!"

❦

Nurse Janet turned to go knock on Principal Hotchkins's door, more to break up his fun than anything else, but as she walked up, she could hear the sounds coming from inside.

"Suck it, bitch!" she heard Principal Hotchkins shouting and wrinkled her nose. The clock read five minutes to ten, she didn't have time for this. Throwing her hands up, she turned around and scribbled a note on a piece of paper on Bobbie's desk. 'Tommy really sick. I've called professionals. Don't open his door.'

"I've got lunch to make," she grumbled and stomped out of the office.

PART III - SAVINI CHARTER SCHOOL

INSIDE THE PRINCIPAL'S OFFICE, he had Bobbie's head gripped between his hands, ramming her up and down between his legs.

"I'm so close," he spat. "Do something besides just holding your mouth open!"

He didn't wait for any kind of reply, he just slammed her head up and down harder and faster. "C'mon!"

"Grr... unnhh," Bobbie grunted.

"Yeah, that's more like it! Make some noise. Choke on my python!"

"Grrrugg."

His forced ramming into her open mouth continued as he neared climax. He grunted himself, so close now, but he needed something to push him over the edge - then he started screaming.

"Ahh!"

He kicked forward, sending Bobbie hurtling against the wall. She hit it with a crunch and fell to her knees, his severed member slipping from her mouth in an ooze of blood and spit.

Principal Hotchkins looked down between his legs as liquid scarlet poured from the little nubbin that remained. "You bitch!"

He pushed himself up on his desk with his left hand and pulled his pants up with his right. Turning away, he stumbled from his office. Blood soaked his underwear and ran down his legs, leaving a crimson trail that zig-zagged toward the nurse's office.

His hand trembled on the locked door handle. Head spinning, he reached into his pocket and pulled out the large ring of school keys and fumbled through them until he found the right one.

Behind the door, the cot lay empty and the small shape of a young boy pawed at the locked entry.

Principal Hotchkins slammed the door open, not noticing the small shape he knocked back against the wall, and limped to the first aid cabinet. He opened it, letting go of his pants, and threw items onto the counter.

"Where the fuck is the gauze?" He slammed his fist on the counter as his pants slumped around his ankles. A small pool of blood formed at his feet from the river rushing from his crotch. Behind the principal, Tommy crawled across the floor, got behind him and took a chunk out of the exposed ankle.

"Ahhh!" the principal cried out, spun around and slipped in his own pooling blood.

BOBBIE SAT on the floor in the principal's office, thoughtlessly masticating on the fleshy member she'd picked up off the floor after Principal Hotchkins had fled. Her jaw moved up and down, her lips stained with crimson. She swallowed his python with a gurgling squish and then perked her head up as faint sounds from down the hall stirred her hunger. She stood, shuffling in the direction of the conference room.

As she passed the nurse's open office door, a bloody-faced Tommy emerged and followed her. A few moments later a half-naked and very bloody Principal Hotchkins also followed. They arrived together at the closed door, from behind which many voices were coming and started clawing at it.

The PTA conference was ready to begin.

❧

10:20AM

The brothers' red Prius pulled to a stop in front of the school, the electric engine of the car turning off automatically.

"I'll never get used to that," Jonah said.

"I know what you mean," Judas nodded as he turned the ignition off and removed the keys. "It sure is easier to drive than Sasha though."

Jonah opened his door, "True, but once you learn on a stick, you'll be able to drive anything."

"How long until she's fixed, do ya think?" Judas asked as he stepped from the car.

"A while. She's in pretty bad shape after that tumble at Winter Oaks. Besides all the body damage, the tranny's shot."

"I miss her."

"Yeah, me too." Jonah looked at his little brother, nodding. "Pop the trunk and let's load up."

"Jonah, we can't take our guns in there. It's a school." Judas reached up and adjusted his hat.

"So?"

"It's filled with kids. It's against the law."

"If we don't take our guns, it will be filled with zombies."

"Is that against the law?"

Jonah looked at Judas and raised an eyebrow. "What?"

"Well, having a firearm on the school grounds is a felony."

"Fine. Leave yours here. There's bail money in the shoebox on top of my dresser."

"Which one?"

"Which one what?"

"Which shoebox, Nike or Reebok?" Judas asked.

"Nike."

"Ok, good." Judas put his gun on the seat and closed his door.

Jonah stared at him. "What do you mean, good?"

"Well," Judas stammered, "JJ and I spent the money in the Reebok's box."

"You what?" Jonah glowered.

"I can't tell you."

Jonah's hand swung to his head, rubbing his temple. "You can't tell me?"

"No."

"Why not?"

"It's a surprise. We ordered you something."

Jonah's mouth hung open. "You what?"

"You can't tell JJ I told you. She'll be pissed if she knew the surprise was ruined."

"What surprise?"

"Jonah, please!"

Jonah studied his brother, then nodded. "Ok, but make sure neither of you ever touch the Nike box unless it's for bail."

"Sure thing, Jonah."

"And while we're at it, don't touch the money taped to the underside of my dresser, either."

Judas cocked his head to the side. "What do you mean, under your dresser? When did you start that?"

Jonah laughed. "Right after we met JJ. I had a feeling doubling our bail stash might be necessary. That woman's a fireball."

"A beautiful fireball," Judas blurted, then laughed. "But yeah, you're probably right."

The phone in Jonah's back pocket let out a beep.

"What was that?" Judas asked.

"I don't know, I've never heard it make that kind of noise before." He pulled it out and looked at the screen.

1 New Message

"It says I have a new message."

"Who's it from, Jonah?"

He clicked the button that said 'read message' and read it aloud. "It's from JJ. Hi cuties! Be safe and don't get into any trouble without me."

Judas laughed, "She knows us pretty well already, huh?"

Jonah clicked at buttons on his phone.

"What are you doing?"

"Trying to send a reply."

Judas watched as Jonah pushed button after button on the flip phone. "You heard what she said, she doesn't want us getting in trouble without her!"

Jonah glanced at his brother with a glare and continued pushing buttons. Finally, he slapped it shut and put it away in his pocket. He undid the buckle on Brutus's holster and put his trusty revolver on the floor of the car, locked the door and headed toward the school.

"What did you say back, Jonah?"

"I said, Ok."

"Ok? That's it?"

"Yeah, that was it."

"But what about all those buttons you pressed?"

"That's how many buttons it took to type it."

"You need a new phone, Jonah."

They walked up the stairs toward the school's front door.

"What did she say the principal's name was?"

"Mr. Hotchkins."

"I bet he's a strict principal."

Jonah gave him a sideways glance. "What makes you say that?"

"Kids make fun of a name like that. Hootchykins. Hot Chickens."

"Hot chickens?" Jonah rolled his eyes and shook his head.

"Yeah." Judas nodded like it was an obvious conclusion.

"And you think that scarred him for life?"

"It would me." Judas spat out his chew and, getting a curious eye raise from Jonah, explained, "No tobacco on campus, plus I need to quit."

Jonah threw his hands into the air as they approached the school entrance. "When did you start paying attention enough to learn what was legal at schools - and why would you need to quit?"

"They have signs everywhere, Jonah. See?" he pointed directly ahead of them to the front door where a big sign in yellow read, 'No Firearms, Drugs, Alcohol or Tobacco allowed on school premises.' It was next to another sign which read, 'Halloween Party 10/29'. Judas ignored the second half of Jonah's question and slipped a hard white candy into his mouth.

Jonah shook his head. "They certainly take the fun out of school these days."

"Not really," Judas pulled a machete from a pocket of his cargo pants. "They don't say nothing about knives."

Jonah stared at the twelve inch blade Judas held before him. "How can you think that's okay?"

Judas opened the front door and held it open with his foot, he waved Jonah through the entrance. "I'll keep it hidden." He lifted his shirt, slid the blade down the inside of his pants and put his shirt over the hilt. "I'm just glad Halloween is still two weeks away."

Jonah stepped inside the quiet school hallway, passing through the metal detectors, and headed toward the sign marked 'Office' a little ways down on the left. "We wouldn't be here if it was Halloween. We'd be holed up at home, ignoring all the pranksters calling our number. Plus, you've got your driving test November 1st."

Judas followed. "I know that, no way in hell we are exterminating on Halloween. I'm not going to jail for shooting someone in zombie make-up, again." He adjusted the hilt of the knife so it was less visible under his shirt. "There Jonah, see, it's out of sight. No one will even notice." He passed through the metal detector.

BRANG! BRANG! A loud metallic alarm sounded and red lights flashed up and down the hallway.

"Oh crap!"

Jonah turned, glaring. "Judas! What did you do?"

Judas pulled the knife back out from under his shirt. "What do I do, Jonah?"

"Quick, toss it back outside!"

Judas opened the door and tossed the blade onto the steps.

The alarm continued.

BRANG!

"Crap, that didn't work," Judas said.

The noise from the alarm down-shifted, becoming quieter, but continuing. A head popped out from a classroom down the hall, looked at the brothers and disappeared again.

"Better just pick it back up, Judas. The lights aren't on for the metal detectors. I think that's for something else."

An automated voice sounded over the loud speakers. "School lockdown commencing. Return to your classrooms or report to a safe room immediately. Remain calm and await further instructions." There was a series of bolts clicking as classroom doors locked automatically and then silence as the alarm became only the flashing red lights lining the hallways.

Judas turned to go back out the door, but as he did so, there was a loud rattle. A metal barrier slid down from above them.

"Lockdown in progress," the automated voice said.

The barrier slammed shut right in front of Judas, cutting off the light from outside. Similar barriers slid down over windows and doors around the school. Soon, the brothers found themselves standing in a dimly lit hallway with nothing but the flashing red alarm lights.

"Let's get to the office," Jonah said. "We need to find out what's going on."

They rushed down the hallway, but came to a stop as they saw blood smeared hand prints on the window in the door. The door was sliding open. Crawling from the room, hands covered in blood, a short thick brunette woman pulled her body through the entryway. Clutching onto her left leg, a young girl, no older than ten, with sunken skin, a bloody face and blond hair in pigtails, gnawed on the woman's ankle.

"Ah—, get it off me!" the woman cried.

Judas stepped over the brunette's body, whose screams echoed down the empty hallways. He grabbed the little blonde girl by the pigtails and yanked her off the woman.

The brunette screamed even louder as the little girl scratched at the woman's legs trying to hold onto her meal, but she only managed to tear a chunk of calf free, instead.

Judas held the girl before him in the air by her pigtails. Her face carried a green pallor and blood dripped from her chin. Her small mouth gnawed on the chunk of flesh as she tried to twist around for Judas.

"Jonah?" Judas looked at his brother, "She's..."

"Yea..." Jonah too was at a loss for words.

"Help me," the brunette said, grasping at the gushing wound on her leg. "They came in the conference room and started biting people. I think they killed them all!"

"Who did?" Jonah asked.

"Principal Hotchkins, that bimbo receptionist and one of the students. They came through the door right as Mr. Ross, the art teacher, turned to say something and Principal Hotchkins just bit right into his neck. Blood sprayed everywhere. I made it out and went to hide in a closet, but," she stopped and pointed at the little monster now grasping and trying to turn on Judas, "that thing was in there waiting for me."

She lost her train of thought for a moment and stared at the blood running from her leg. "What possessed them to do this? Why?" She looked back up at Judas. "What's the matter with them?"

Judas stared at her, uncertain what to say or do. Her skin was pale and taking on the same green tint as the girl in his arms.

"I got out and hit the lockdown button in the office, but she was clinging to my leg."

"Ma'am," Jonah bent down next to her and took her hand in his. "Where is this conference room?"

She looked at him, the light in her eyes dimming, lids fluttering. "Down the hall at the back of the office."

Judas, who still held the little blonde zombie by her pigtails, pushed the door open with his hip and scooted into the office to glance down the hall. The conference room door stood open, inside was a bloodbath.

PART IV - KICK BALL

INSIDE THE CONFERENCE ROOM, Tommy's small form knelt beside
the body of a bald man with a rotund belly who lay on the floor.
The boy had his hands deep inside the fallen man's abdomen, his
right hand emerged, tugging a long tubular piece of intestine. He
stuck it in his mouth and chewed on it with zeal.

Further past him, a woman's body sat up, eyes closed. Freshly
turned, Judas thought. The little girl hanging from her pigtails in
his hands groaned and reached up to grab at him but came up
short. The woman's eyes popped open at the sound and she
growled in Judas's direction. A mass of shadows within the conference room danced along the wall behind her.

"Jonah!" Judas stepped back into the hall and saw his brother
kneeling down beside the now motionless woman. "Crap," he
muttered, then spoke up. "Jonah, there's a bunch of 'em and I think
they know we're here."

Jonah looked up. "We need to find some weapons."

"But where?"

"Maybe there's something we can use in the office."

"Like what, a stapler?"

"Let's take a look."

"Ok, but there's not much time. They're coming. What do I do with this one?" He lifted her a little higher by her pigtails.

"Use her as a shield and push them back down the hall, try to buy us some time."

The brothers entered the office and walked behind the counter. Looking down the hall they could see the newly turned woman using the wall to pull herself to her feet. Two dead men were already on their way. The boy still ate.

Jonah opened drawer after drawer. Stationary, rubber bands, paper clips, not so much as a sharpened pencil. He glanced up as the shapes from down the hall neared Judas. "Nothing yet, keep them back!"

Judas set the girl down and grabbed her arms, pushing them to her sides and using his large hands to pin them against her. He picked her back up and ran at the nearest man, knocking him back.

"If this is all there is, we might be able to contain this by keeping them in here," Judas shouted, backing up to evaluate what might happen next. More shapes were crowding into the doorway and the man's body the young boy ate from sat up and rolled over, tugging the piece of intestine from the child zombie's grasp.

The boy reached up and yanked on it, pulling out a couple more wet, red feet, shoving them in his mouth and grasping the rest like he was doing a rope climb. The large man stood and walked toward Judas. The boy stayed put a moment as several feet of entrails pulled free, then the momentum of the man yanked him forward.

Jonah opened a drawer at the receptionist's desk and rummaged through it. He pulled out a large pair of scissors and set them on the counter next to a large commercial paper cutter. The next drawer included fashion magazines and a bag of candy, and finally a sharpened jumbo pencil. He set it on the counter as well and opened the bottom drawer which included a purse and, for a moment, he thought it held promise. Ever since they had met JJ, they had learned a lot about all the places a woman could hide a gun. Unfortunately, the only potential weapon it contained was a can of mace, which he'd never thought to try before on a zombie but doubted it would do much good.

He looked up and saw Judas pushing the bald man with the spewing large intestine back with the pig-tailed shield. Behind the fat zombie, quite a few forms moved into the space. "There's not enough to use here." Jonah grabbed the scissors and held them up. "Just these and a jumbo sized pencil; they won't work on fresh skulls very well, only through the eyes, ears and base of the skull."

The throng of zombies in the hall surged forward again, rushing at Judas.

A tall thin zombie with glasses and a blood soaked dress shirt charged past the fat zombie with the hole in his stomach but tripped over the taut-trail of intestines. They stretched all the way back to the boy who remained in the conference room. The fat zombie growled as the force of it pulled another long stretch of tubular flesh and blood from inside him. He looked around, slamming a fist against the wall.

The tripped zombie fell at Judas's feet. Judas stepped back, bumping against the counter and almost dropping the little girl gnawing at the air in his arms.

"Bro, it's time to roll. We gotta go."

Jonah slammed a drawer shut. "Dammit!"

The fat zombie lumbered forward and Judas sidestepped, slamming the little girl's body against the undead giant's meaty arm. Judas shoved, knocking the hulking form over. The zombie screeched as it fell, a large mass of intestine bursting out from the hole, liquid and ooze splattering on the floor.

Judas and the little girl fell forward, carried by the momentum of his thrust. His feet slipped in the muck and they ended up in a dog pile, with Judas on top.

"Aww crap!" Jonah saw the calamity and grabbed the scissors from the counter top.

The zombies in the hall tripped over the tall thin one that had fallen and were piling up. That bought them a moment, but trouble was getting close. The big zombie was on his side with the little girl pressed up against his arm, pinning it down. Her head twisted at an odd angle, very near Judas's own arm. She nipped and growled at him.

Jonah reached down and grabbed Judas by the shoulder, pulled him up, and shoved the blades of the scissors into the girl's ear, silencing her. As he pulled them out, a green slime covered the blades and oozed out of her ear. Jonah's eyes shot open and he dropped the scissors, which clacked onto the floor.

Judas, just regaining his footing, looked down at the ooze. "Oh crap. Is that what I think it is?"

"It sure looks like it. Don't touch it and make sure none gets on you."

"This just went from bad to worse," Judas said. "I thought all of that green poison had been destroyed!"

"I thought so too, but there must've been more than what was at the plant when we—" he turned and shouted at Judas. "Look out!"

The conference room zombies were right next to them. A short, dark haired woman with half her face missing, loose skin flapping against her cheek bone, grabbed Judas's arm and lunged at it, teeth bared.

Judas fell back, colliding into Jonah, and both brothers tumbled into the cramped space behind the receptionist desk. The dark haired zombie fell with them, mouth open, gnashing at the bill of Judas's baseball cap. A half dozen more recently turned and very hungry dead were fast on her heels.

She pulled forward, trying to dig into his flesh, but only managing to pull the cap off his head and cover his face.

"Push up!" Jonah shouted, "I'm pinned under you!"

Judas shoved upward on the woman's small frame, lifting her and his hat off him. She dropped the hat from her teeth and growled. He rolled to his side taking her with him while scooping his hat up and freeing Jonah from underneath.

Jonah scrambled to his feet, pulling Judas up too. "Keep her away from you!"

Judas put his hat on backward and grabbed the biting woman and spun her around to face the oncoming dead.

They were now trapped behind the receptionist's desk. The group from the conference room pressed directly behind the short dark haired woman, grasping around and trying to get a piece of the brothers.

"What are we gonna do Jonah? I don't like being the middle of this sandwich!"

Jonah looked around. From the other side of the desk to the door, it was wide open. The desk was tall, littered with forms and the large paper cutter. "If we can get over the counter, we can get outta here!" Jonah shouted in his brother's ear as he helped push the woman away.

"We can't both make it, Jonah! Go for it, I'll hold them back."

"No way I'm going without you, brother. On three, let's give her a shove and see if we can push this crowd back."

"You got it," Judas said, straining as sweat dripped down his forehead.

"You're closer to them, so you go first, Judas. Slip under my arm then over the counter."

"But—"

"One!" Jonah shouted.

"Jonah—"

"Two!"

"You—"

"Three!"

They shoved forward into the woman and met the weight of half a dozen hungry flesh-eaters pushing back against them. Only creating about a foot of space from where they had been, but it was enough.

"Go!" Jonah shouted.

Judas didn't hesitate to do as he was told. Judas knew not doing so would mean death for them both, but fear for his brother kept him from going far. He ducked down under Jonah's arm and jumped onto the receptionist counter, but instead of jumping off it to safety, he stormed down it, yelling and kicking at the zombies massed there.

Jonah found himself pushed back against the wall, the dead woman and the force of those behind her pinning him. He could feel hands tugging at his coat, trying to dig into his flesh. He had one hand pressed against the woman's back and the other pushing her head forward so she couldn't turn and bite him.

"C'mon, get off him and get at me!" Judas yelled.

The weight shifted as those crowded behind turned to grasp at Judas on the counter top. Jonah found he could push the woman back to an arm's length, then Judas was shouting beside him.

"Put her head in here!"

Jonah looked over and saw Judas turning the large paper cutter so that the blade side was closest to Jonah. He got what his brother was doing and smiled. He tightened his hands on the woman's blouse and slammed her head to the side, smacking it against the green metal platform of the cutter, her neck lying underneath the blade.

Judas's boot came up and slammed down on the handle.

K-thunk!

The woman's head, still gnashing and biting, rolled off the side of the counter.

"How's that for a science project?" Judas grinned. "Homemade guillotine! Wouldn't Mr. Benson be proud?"

Jonah laughed despite the peril of their situation, remembering their middle school science project that had almost gotten them expelled. One of many, actually, that had gotten them into trouble. He shoved the lifeless body back and made some space.

"You sure got his attention when you exploded our beer-fueled volcano all over the classroom."

"Hey, that wasn't my fault, I was distracted!" Judas jumped down from the counter, narrowly missing the zombie head. He kicked it out of the way and it rolled toward the small doorway that separated the office from the lobby. The group coming down the hallway split in two, pushing the half door open and knocking the woman's head back toward Judas.

"Distracted?" Jonah yelled as he climbed up on to the counter. "We were at the most important step!" He jumped down and turned back, grabbing the sharpened pencil off the counter.

"Yeah, distracted," Judas said, kicking the head away from him again. "By Bobbie, remember her?"

Jonah shook his head. "You mean Bobbie Burns?"

"Yeah, you remember she always teased me and introduced herself as 'Bobbie' with one O and then she'd squeeze her tits together and say 'and two B's'."

"Oh yeah, how could I forget her?"

They moved toward the office door.

"Well, she'd turned around in her chair, she'd dropped one of those lollipops she was always sucking on and bent over; I poured the whole can in before I knew it."

Jonah opened the door and was greeted by the lunging form of the dead brunette they'd left in the hallway. He collided with her and swung the large pencil up, shoving it right through her eye. They tumbled forward in a mass of limbs and noise. "Close the door, Judas! Close the door!"

Judas turned and grabbed the door handle to swing it closed, but as he did so, the head of the dark haired woman shot forward, kicked by the mass of zombies. It rolled right into the doorway and stopped the door from closing. Before he could do anything, the dead rushed through the opening. He turned and pulled Jonah to his feet. They scrambled away to the intersection where the school halls connected.

The angry rolling head followed close behind as it was once again, kicked, in their direction by the approaching zombies.

THE LOPPED off head rolled to a stop at Jonah's feet, biting at his boot.

"We need to find some weapons!" Jonah said, kicking the dead head back toward the zombies coming at them.

"If only we had more of those giant pencils, they did the job!"

"We're gonna need better weapons than that."

"Yeah, but where are we gonna find those inside a school?"

"I don't know," Jonah said, "but I'm gonna call JJ and see if she can get over here stat." He reached toward his back pocket where the shape of his flip phone bulged out.

"HEY!" a loud voice rang out behind them.

The brothers turned to see a heavy-set woman in a blood-smeared apron coming toward them, a rolling pin in her meaty hand.

Primal fear took over as their minds processed the image before them. A moment in time from long ago played out in both their heads.

Jonah, *Judas and their friends had sat huddled around the lunch table, talking, laughing and eating. Someone challenged Judas to see how high he could fling a grape with the trebuchet he'd made. No one remembered who had made the challenge, but it had actually been Judas's own suggestion.*

He'd made the trebuchet for the school science fair and had been dying to show it off. He'd gotten it out of his locker to take to Mr. Benson's class after lunch. It was the first of their experiments to go wrong, but not the last.

They'd started by flinging a grape across the room. It had gone high and bounced off the far wall to uproarious laughter from their friends. A second grape delivered similar results, but by the third Judas knew he would have to kick it up a notch.

"This is getting boring," he said. "What else can we launch?"

Everyone spoke, offering pieces of their lunch and declaring how great it would be to see this or that fly through the air. Then Allan, a ninth grader, handed over his dessert. "I dare you to see how far you can fling this."

The table grew silent. Everyone knew it was a bad idea, but Allan had used the one word guaranteed to get them into trouble: 'Dare'.

Jonah grabbed his brother by the collar and whispered in his ear. "Aim it toward the bathrooms." There was no one over in that area, the rest of the room was packed with kids, eating, laughing and enjoying themselves.

"Good idea Bro!"

He balanced the cup of pudding in the bucket and pulled the lever back until it clicked into place.

"Ready?" he whispered as the whole table fell quiet around him, followed by other tables as they sensed something happening. Little did the brothers or their friends know but part of the reason was because Beatrice Putnam, school lunch lady, having witnessed their grape-scapades, was lumbering up behind them. Her large form didn't allow her to move too fast, so she didn't make it in time to stop him.

Click!

Judas hit the lever that released the bucket's catapulting arm.

The arm flung the pudding, but not up and away like they had hoped, just straight up and over a little. The container flipped end over end, spraying out its contents into a giant brown puddle. It struck the tiled ceiling and hung there for just a moment before raining down in large globs.

Kids from the table next to them cried out as the pudding landed like chocolate water balloons on top of them, splashing across the table, covering their hair and faces and ruining what remained of their lunches.

Judas's friends busted out laughing and the kids from the pudding-bombarded table glared in their direction. They pointed at Judas and his trebuchet and then picked up handfuls of their own food, fists raised.

It was on!

In moments, the cafeteria was pandemonium as everything imaginable became a messy missile in a war that most hadn't even seen start.

A hot dog, sans bun, but slobbering catsup, whirled past Judas, followed by a half dozen potato projectiles, before Jonah grabbed him. "Get down!" Jonah yanked his younger brother by the sleeve. They ducked beneath the table as all around them the floor became littered with half eaten debris. A bologna sandwich there, half a banana, peel-and-all there, random gummy bears everywhere and then a pair of cold clammy hands wrapped around each of their juvenile necks.

They were lifted so fast and the rush of air in their ears was so loud, they felt like they were being abducted by aliens.

"Jonah and Judas Zee, what the hell have you done? You pair of good-for-nothing troublemakers!" She jerked them towards the cafeteria exit. "You're going to the principal's office!" She dragged them face first, doubled over, as the food-storm they had unleashed continued in a downpour around them.

Once outside the chaos of the lunchroom, she bent down and pulled both of their faces in close to hers. "Do you boys believe in Jesus?"

"Yes ma'am," they sputtered.

"Good, cause after that god-awful mess you just made in there, you better start praying you never end up on school assistance and have to have hot lunch, cause if you do, I'm gonna serve you The Lunch Lady

Special!" She stopped there and looked them both in the eyes, one after the other, deliberately raising her eyebrows as she did so, then she burst out in a cackle.

Jonah tried to shake free of her vice-like grip, resulting in Miss Putnam squeezing even harder on their necks.

"Wanna know what it is?" she asked.

"No," Jonah said, face flushed.

"Too bad," she spat and pulled them in tighter, whispering into their ears.

Their faces grew paler until finally Judas turned away, his mouth hanging open. "That's disgusting," he said, shaking his head.

They got suspended for a week and didn't eat lunch in the cafeteria the rest of the school year. They only saw Miss Putnam one other time in the final days before school let out, it was in the hall near the administration office. She stopped and smiled at them with her face split from side to side in a wide and toothy grin.

"Is it lunch time yet, boys?"

⁂

THE WOMAN STANDING behind the now grown Zee Brothers was not Miss Putnam, but the outfit and general similarities in size and stature was enough to send the primal part of their brains into a panic.

"Who are you and what are you doing here?" the woman barked, raising the rolling pin.

The mass of zombies was just coming into view at the intersection behind them.

Stammering, Jonah said, "We're zombie exterminators."

She squinted at them and then glanced up as the first few dead PTA members rounded the corner. "Not doing a very good job of it, are you?" She paused a moment and backed away from them. "Follow me."

PART VI - NANTUCKET

THEY RAN down the hall putting a dozen yards between them and the slow moving zombies, catching up with the woman in the lunch lady uniform who, despite her bulk, was quite fast.

"We need weapons, ma'am!" Jonah shouted at her.

The woman glanced over her shoulder as she hustled away from the dead. "If you're the exterminators I called, where's your equipment?"

Jonah glared at Judas and answered. "We left it in the car, ma'am."

She shook her head in disbelief. "Why would you do that?"

Jonah opened his mouth to answer, but Judas interjected. "It's illegal, ma'am. I saw all the signs posted outside. We didn't want to get in trouble."

Janet stopped short, right next to a series of vending machines. One for sodas, another for snacks and the final one for school supplies. A big poster was pasted to the side of the first with a headline reading, 'Eat Energy-Os every day to get smarter faster!'. Underneath that in smaller print, it read, 'Energy-Os and Energy-O Drink Additive are recommended for daily use by students by the Incorporated American Education System, A U.C.A. subsidiary.'

She looked the brothers up and down.

Judas still wore the clothes he'd woken up in; dirty jeans with a ripped out knee on the left leg, a wrinkled t-shirt and his ancient, oil stained jean jacket, plus his Diamondbacks hat. Jonah's attire, while newer and a little cleaner, was pretty much identical, minus the hat.

"You two don't look like following rules is a priority."

The brothers glanced at each other; neither had even put on their combat vests before rushing from the house to get to the school.

"We didn't think things would be this far out of control," Jonah said, with a look back.

The zombies came right for them, but slowly, and there was enough distance to leave some breathing room. It looked like at least twenty of them. Not too many, but without the proper equipment the brothers wouldn't be able to handle them.

"Most classrooms will be in lockdown," Janet said. "There's stuff you can use in the kitchen to deal with these things." She turned, walking past a room marked 'Computer Lab', where a young girl cowered underneath a desk.

Judas stopped in front of the snack machine pointing. "Hey Jonah, they got peanut butter cups for only fifty cents! We should get some for JJ!" He grinned.

Jonah raised his eyes. "Really? Now?"

"Well, she said they're her favorite after..." Judas trailed off, blushing.

Jonah shook his head, "Judas, I—"

"Hey, look Jonah. This one has school supplies in it. Even some of those giant pencils. We could sharpen more of those if we need to."

"Ahem," Nurse Janet interrupted from behind them. "We have a kitchen full of knives," she hefted the rolling pin, "and tons of other implements you can use - if you two will quit yammering and follow me."

Jonah glared at Judas again then looked at the cafeteria lady and said, "We're right behind you, ma'am."

Janet turned and stormed away.

Jonah grabbed the hat off Judas's head and smacked him with it, Gilligan-style.

"Let's go," Jonah growled, handing his brother his hat back.

They passed the computer lab and were hot on her heels when a scared voice cried out from behind them.

"Help!"

The trio spun to find a short, dark-skinned girl, with long black-braided hair and wearing white-rimmed glasses, sticking her head out of the door to the room marked 'Computer Lab'.

"Crap," Nurse Janet said. "The automated lockdown only works on designated classrooms, ancillary rooms don't lock."

The zombies drew closer but were far enough away that there wasn't a need to panic, quite yet.

"Judas, go get that kid." Jonah barked at his brother and turned to the lunch lady. "Ma'am go on, we'll catch up or..." he glanced back at the approaching crowd.

"I'll load up and come back, just hold them off," Nurse Janet said, then turned tail and hustled her bulk down the hall.

Jonah turned to see Judas approaching the girl. She'd come far enough out the door to peer past the vending machines and down the hall, seeing the mass of dead adults coming to feast on them.

"What..." she panted, "what are they?"

"They're..." Judas's forehead wrinkled. "I'm not sure how to say it, they're..."

The crowd was close enough now, that she could make out the blood and gore covering their bodies. She let out a squeak and stepped back. "Why are Mr. Hotchkins' pants down? And he's all bloody at the waist." She pointed at the dead principal, who was a dozen paces ahead of the rest and making his way straight for them. The growls and groans of the group were now audible.

"They're zombies, kid," Judas said. "There's some kind of outbreak happening."

"Zombies?" The kid's face turned pale and she retreated into the computer lab.

"No!" Judas reached for her. "Don't go that way. Come with me."

The girl shook her head, backing further into the room. "No, no. I don't wanna get eaten." She fell to her knees and backed underneath a table.

Judas turned to see Jonah, who'd watched as the scene went from bad to worse, and now made his way there.

The computer lab consisted of four rows of ten, split down the middle by a small aisle. Computer desks and big office style computer chairs filled the room. The girl appeared to be the only occupant.

Jonah stepped in beside Judas and whispered in his ear. "Go talk to her. Find out her name. Try and get her to trust you so she'll follow us and leave. I'll see if I can buy us some time."

Judas nodded. "You got it." He walked over to the scared girl and squatted, reaching into his pocket and pulling out two hard mint candies. He unwrapped the first one and popped it in his mouth, then took a deep breath and gave the girl a smile. "I know you're scared. I am too. My name's Judas by the way. What's yours?"

Behind them, the sounds of computer chairs rattling as they were moved and shoved through the open doorway drowned out the groans of the approaching dead.

"Muh, muh," the girl panted, her body shaking as she stared toward the open door. "My name is Nantucket..., but they call me Nat the Nerd."

Judas noticed the girl's backpack next to her, books labeled

Applied Physics, Advanced Computer Science and Robotics, among others, spilled out.

"Hi, Nat. It looks like you take some tough courses." Judas pointed at the physics book. "I used to really enjoy science class."

"Those are just ones I checked out from the library. They don't teach those courses here." The girl took in a deep breath and pushed the books back into her backpack.

"Where's the rest of your classmates?"

Nat glanced up and out of the window, glimpsing Jonah shoving a chair into the hall. "They're all in the bathroom."

Judas glanced around the room, clenching his teeth against the hard candy. "Um, why are they in the bathroom? And where is it?"

She took a deep breath. "It's past the science room. Our fish 'Q' died, and they went to flush him. I... I..." she stuttered again. "I stayed here, cause I was trying to finish the program I was writing." She paused and her eyes got wider. "Did 'Q' come back from the dead?"

"Huh?" Judas broke the candy in half with his teeth. "What? No. Well, I don't think so. That isn't how these things usually work. Here." He held out his hand, offering the other candy in his open palm.

The girl looked at it, then at Judas. "I don't know you."

Judas's mouth twitched. He waited a second and thought how Jonah might handle this situation. He considered tossing her over his shoulder but then thought what JJ might do instead. "Nat, you're right. You don't, and there's not a lot of time right now. My name's Judas, like I said, and that guy over there," he indicated Jonah, who was grabbing more chairs from inside the computer lab and wheeling them out into the hallway, "is my brother Jonah. We're The Zee Brothers, Zombie Exterminators."

Nat gasped, her mouth falling open. "You're zombie exterminators?"

"Yeah," Judas nodded. "We were called to come investigate a

sick kid. Only, by the time we got here, things were already out of hand."

She moved her head and looked Judas over. "Where're your weapons?"

Judas's lips tightened, nostrils flaring and his hand closed over the candy as his nails dug into his palm. "They're in the car. It's a long story."

Nat tugged on her braids and stared at Judas, something in her face changing. "And you came here to help us?"

"Yes." Judas relaxed a little. "We're trying."

"That's really brave." She sniffed back a snotty tear. "I feel safer knowing you're a professional."

Judas chuckled and smiled. "Some days I feel like an amateur, but I'm glad you think we're brave. Now, can you come with me and we can get you out of here?" He held out his free hand.

Nat smiled back. "Sure." She paused for a second. "Can I still have that candy?"

PART VII - MUSICAL CHAIRS

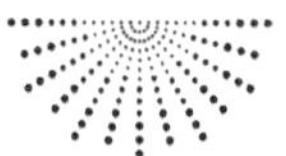

OFFICE CHAIRS and zombies filled the hallway like litter.

Jonah rushed into the room to see Judas and the girl getting up from under the desk.

"Help me grab these chairs. They're slowing them down and creating a bottleneck."

"You got it!" Judas said, grabbing the chair nearest him. "C'mon Nat, can you give us a hand?"

The girl's eyes widened at that and Judas tossed her the candy from his hand. "Sure," she smiled. "I'll help!"

Judas and Nantucket grabbed chairs from around the room and sent them flying across the carpet to the door. Jonah took them and flung them into the tiled hallway. Within moments, they had the room empty of chairs.

Judas walked to the entrance and looked out. The zombies stood bunched in a cluster on the other side of the vending machines and behind the tangle of chairs. It made an excellent barricade, with some chairs tipped over and the crowd of undead pushing against them causing them to move as one connected mass.

Jonah held them in place by shoving against the chairs with his full weight. However, a few of the dead were crawling through the mess and one was making his way along the wall on the farside.

"Help me push them to the side and pin that one to the wall!" Jonah shouted at his brother.

Judas looked at the tangle of chairs and zombies. Seeing three of them crowded next to the side near the vending machines he said, "If we move them that way, these three will get through."

Jonah bit his lip. "We need to figure something out!" He looked at the vending machines, saw a giant sharpened pencil in the display window, and a light went on in his head. He reached for his wallet, pulled it out and tossed it to Judas. "Here, it's like the Mystery Box, buy some of those pencils. We can use them to take a few out as they make their way around."

Judas smiled. "Great idea, Jonah!" He opened his brother's wallet and pulled out two dollar bills. "Um, Jonah, you've only got two bucks."

"Crap, how much are the pencils?"

"Two dollars."

The lone zombie, a tall thin man with half of his neck ripped out and blood staining his blue cardigan sweater, rounded the barricades corner and ambled toward Jonah. "Buy it!"

Jonah looked at the zombie, then at Judas and the girl. "What's your name?"

The girl pressed up against the wall, backpack in one hand, answered in a shaking voice. "My name's Nantucket."

Judas got the first dollar fed into the machine but the second one, an old wrinkly bill, kept getting spat back out. He tried flattening it by rubbing it against the corner of the vending machine.

"Nantucket, I need your help," Jonah said, turning his attention back to the approaching corpse. "I need you to come hold these chairs. Keep pushing them back and keep *them*," he indicated the throng of dead milling about on the other side of the chairs, "from getting at us."

"I... I," the girl stuttered and stayed frozen.

The cardigan-wearing zombie dove for Jonah, who gave the mass of chairs a hard shove and stepped out of the zombie's reach. It stumbled passed him and he grabbed the smaller form by the biceps and held him in place.

"Judas!" Jonah shouted

"I'm trying, bro!" He held up the wrinkly bill and fed it into the machine again.

It went all the way in and for a moment looked as if it would be accepted. The machine whirred for an impossibly long instant, before spitting it back out, this time with one corner bent.

Judas cursed, removed the dollar, straightened it and fed it in again. The machine whirred for the briefest of moments and the bill disappeared. The little digital window read $2.00 and Judas shouted. "Woohoo!" He pressed button A2 and turned to Jonah. "We're gonna need more money if we want any more weapons from this box."

Sweat dripped from Jonah's forehead as he wrestled to keep the zombie in front of him pinned.

The 'thunk' of delivery sounded from the vending machine. "Almost, Jonah!" Judas yelled as he bent and twisted his arm to get inside the plastic tray. He pulled the pencil out, prepared to rush to Jonah's aid, then stopped. "Uh, Jonah, we got a problem. Evidently, that one is only for display. We're gonna need a Pack-a-Punch!"

Jonah turned and looked at his brother, who held a large pencil like they'd seen in the display window, only it wasn't sharpened. Jonah's eyes widened as he took in the situation. They were running out of options. "Get ready to run, we're gonna have to fall back."

"Wait," Nat said. "There's a sharpener in the computer lab." She held out her hand to Judas.

Judas grinned. "Perfect!" He handed Nat the pencil. "Get it as sharp as you can, quick!" He turned back to his brother and rushed to help him. Together they grabbed 'blue cardigan' by the back of his sweater and tossed him over the barricade to where the other hungering dead were massed. He made it most of the way, before landing with a smash, scattering some of the chairs and creating a ruckus amongst the zombies.

"Here, hold the chairs Judas!"

Jonah stepped back, tracking another of the zombies that was making its way around the far side, and grabbed his flip phone from his back pocket. He opened it and held down the number one button until speed dial kicked in.

"Who you calling, Jonah?"

"JJ! We're gonna need back-up!"

PART VIII - DIRTY LAUNDRY

"Hɪ, you've reached JJ! I'm out doing something I probably shouldn't be right now. Leave me a message and if I'm not in jail, I'll get back to you!" The message broke into giggles, then she added, "Life's short, live a little!"

"JJ, this is Jonah. We could use some help. By the time we got here things were… out of control. Our tools got left in the car and we're kinda scrambling here!"

"Tell her I said hi," Judas's voice interrupted the message.

"Dammit Judas, not now. Oh, and JJ, please stop by the garage and grab the box labeled 'gas masks' from Judas's room, I think we're gonna need them." There was a pause and then, "Hurry up with that pencil!"

The screen on JJ's phone, which sat on the dash of her car outside of Xanadu's groomers, flashed '1 New Message From Mr. Z."

JJ sᴛᴏᴏᴅ at the counter inside 'Fluffy Puppies', breathing in

Xanadu's freshly shampooed scent, and admiring the red and black of the new Arizona Diamondback's bandana wrapped around his neck. "The brothers are gonna love that!" She clipped a small white tag, marked with the word, 'iDog' on his collar and adjusted it so that his diamond-plated name tag was visible and smiled.

Rose, the groomer, turned her head to the side and leaned forward, smiling. "Brothers? What exactly have you been up to, JJ?"

JJ's cheeks flushed crimson. She opened her mouth to speak but stopped herself by biting her lip.

Rose's smile widened. "What is it JJ? I'm just like a hairdresser, you can tell me anything! Spill it!" She waited a moment, then coaxed some more, "C'mon."

"I'm kinda dating these two guys." JJ's grin was as wide as could be as she shrugged her shoulders and waited for Rose's reaction.

"You're dating brothers?" Rose's eyes popped open and her voice jumped an octave.

JJ's head nodded, face beaming. "Mhm."

"Oh my god! JJ Hembrook! I can't believe you." Rose giggled. "Do they know?"

JJ started to answer, then Rose's mouth fell open and she blurted out the real question she wanted the answer to. "Are you sleeping with them?"

Looking down and shaking her head, JJ stroked Xanadu's fur. "Yes, they know." She twisted Xanadu's hair in her fingers, "and no... not yet."

Rose leaned halfway across the counter, her grin so wide it hurt. "Are you going to?" and before JJ could respond, "which one?" Her hand flew up, covering her mouth. "Oh my God, I'm so sorry. I can't help myself!" She laughed and shook her head, then looked up, waiting.

JJ giggled back. "I don't know, maybe both."

"Oh, you little slut!" Rose burst out and doubled over laughing.

Their faces were bright red as they tried to catch their breath between fits of giggles. Xanadu sat on the counter between them, his head lowered.

"What are they like? Are they cute?"

"They are both rugged and handsome. Jonah's the older one, he's more serious, confident, in-charge, he always has a plan. Judas is," she paused, a funny smile forming on her face. "I don't know, he's just fun, easy going, a little silly. He makes me laugh and he tries so hard it's adorable."

They chatted a bit more, laughing and smiling, then it was time to pay the bill and go.

"Ok, now that I've shared all my dirty laundry, let me take Xanadu outside and see if I can get him to poop so I can pay my bill."

"That sure is some dog!" Rose scratched the top of Xanadu's head, and he rose like a cat to greet the thrusting fingers. "Make sure and get messy again soon Xanadu, so you can come back and I can hear what your dirty little momma is up to next."

Outside, JJ set Xanadu on the grass next to her Charger. "Ok boy, do your business." She reached in and grabbed her cigarettes and phone off the dash. Her perma-smile grew wider as she saw the missed call and message from Jonah. She lit her cigarette, pulled a small black plastic baggy from her pocket and turned to watch her fur baby.

Xanadu piddled a little here and a little there as he wandered around the small patch of grass smelling the scents of his wolf brothers. Finally, finding the right spot, he squatted and pushed out a tiny black nugget, shook his hiney, and trotted off sniffing at the air.

JJ pulled the little black bag over her hand and scooped up the sparkling doggie doo. She tied the bag off and held her phone up to her ear, pressing play on the voicemail.

Xanadu wandered around the grassy patch following new scents, then stopped short, head raising, a low growl in his throat.

Across the street from the parking lot, a white van sat parked next to the curb. There were no windows on it and the only markings were a faded and obscured symbol inside a circle near the back. In the driver's window, the face of a large man with short blonde hair in a military cut eyed JJ.

Xanadu opened his mouth to bark when JJ swooped him up, wrapping her arm around his waist.

"C'mon boy, we gotta go!"

She hopped in the car, tossed Xanadu on the passenger seat, opened the over-crowded glove box and threw the little black baggy inside. "I'll deal with that later."

The Charger peeled out of the parking lot and shot down the road.

The man in the van watched her go.

***

"Why'd you tell her to get the gas masks, Jonah?"

"That green tint to the zombie's skin… especially the young ones they called about getting sick first. We've seen that before and this started somewhere, we've got to find the source of it."

"Gotcha," Judas nodded. "How could it be, though? We torched that place when we left. It should've all been destroyed."

"I don't know, Judas. It's a large corporation. Dr. Nitsau could've had other facilities where the gas was stored."

"Here!" Nat appeared out of the computer lab with the jumbo pencil sharpened to a fine point. "Will this work?"

Judas pushed against the mass of chairs and grinned. "Yeah Nat, that's perfect. Give it to my brother!"

Jonah stood near the far side of the chair barricade, toying with the tall skinny zombie. He'd been pushing a chair into it, keeping it back while they waited. So far, their impromptu obstruction had worked rather well.

Nat took the tiniest of steps as she watched Jonah and the

zombie, making her way to him. "Here you go, Mr. Jonah." She held up the pencil.

The tall skinny zombie growled as Jonah removed one hand from the chair and grabbed the pencil. "Thanks, kid!" Jonah shoved the chair out of the way and used the lumbering corpse's momentum to knock it to the ground. He climbed on its back, grabbed it by the hair and rammed the sharpened pencil through its tympanic membrane.

The body went slack beneath him. He pulled the pencil out part way, saw a green ooze around it and pushed it back in. The gooey liquid continued to drip out from around the punctured ear. He reached down and pulled out the man's wallet, saw there were bills in it, and handed it to Nat. "Here, give this to Judas."

Nat took the wallet and stared at the pencil protruding from the dead man's head. "That's awesome!"

Jonah stood up, looking at the girl, and crinkling his brow. "He was human only a few minutes ago." He looked the girl in the eyes. "We only do this because it's kill or be killed. To stop this from getting out of control."

Nantucket blinked, eyes watering. "Sorry, Mr. Jonah. I've never seen anything like that before. They're scary, but to see you do that, to know they can be stopped, it takes the scary away."

Jonah smiled. "Get that wallet to Judas and let's dispatch some more of these walking cadavers."

"You got it!" Nat grinned. She turned and rushed over to where Judas waited near the vending machines.

The zombies on the other side of the chairs growled and groaned but made little progress toward them. A couple had even turned and gone back down the hall. A few more, trying to crawl between the chair legs, found themselves stuck in the tangled mess, they groaned and grasped fruitlessly at the air.

Jonah took a deep breath, reached into his pocket for a cigar and cursed, remembering where they were. Two women from the crowd of dead broke off and made their way toward the gap along the wall. One was tall and skinny and wearing a dress, the other was short and rather large; she might be a challenge. He turned to check on Judas and Nat's progress and his mouth fell open. "Judas!!"

Judas had taken the wallet from Nantucket, pulled out the money and counted it. It contained ten dollars. A five and five ones. He fed the five into the school supply vending machine, purchased two jumbo pencils and handed them to Nat for sharpening. He glanced over his shoulder, saw Jonah eyeing the zombies and fed a dollar into the snack machine.

The peanut butter cups were in slot C4, but in his rush to buy them before anyone noticed, he hit C3 and a one dollar package of Energy-Os drink powder dispensed instead. "Dammit," he muttered and fed another dollar into the machine. His anxious finger pressed C4 just as Jonah shouted his name.

Judas spun. His brother glared. The crowd of zombies groaned.

"What are you doing?" Jonah's face was tight and red, his jaw clenched.

Judas grimaced and bit his lip, blushing. He looked up at Jonah. "You're just mad you didn't think of it!"

Jonah threw his hands into the air. "I can't believe you!"

Judas looked at the floor and shifted his feet.

"How much is left?"

Judas held up three dollar bills. "Plus there's still a dollar in the supply vending machine."

"Buy a damn pair of scissors already!" Jonah pointed to where one of the crawlers was nearing Judas's position.

"Oh shit!" Judas fed the money into the machine.

Nat appeared in the door with a sharpened pencil. "Your personal Pack-a-Punch at your service!" She tossed the pencil to Jonah and disappeared back into the computer lab.

Judas bent and grabbed the scissors from the first machine, then slipped his hand into the snack machine. He pulled out the two packages and shoved them into his inside coat pocket.

Jonah goaded the tall thin female toward him. "Come on, come and get some."

The zombie growled and came at him, the large heavy set zombie close on her heels.

Judas watched as the zombie crawling through the chairs grew close enough. He grabbed the man's hair, yanked him forward and shoved the scissors into his ear. That same bloody-green discharge poured out as the corpse went slack. Judas pulled out the scissors, wiped them clean on the dead man's shirt, and stood.

In the computer lab doorway, Nat was back with another sharpened jumbo pencil at the ready.

Jonah rammed the first pencil into the thin woman's eye socket and her body slumped to the ground. The large heavyset woman tripped over the corpse, stumbled, and fell into the tangle of chairs, scattering them. The zombies stuck on the other side growled and lunged as the chairs shifted.

Judas grabbed the pencil from Nat and tossed it to Jonah. "Maybe we ought to get into vampire slaying too! Making stakes seems pretty easy."

Jonah caught the pencil. "No, let's leave that to Irish and the Gunns. It takes more than a pile of sticks to get that job done."

"Yeah, you're right," Judas said. "Besides, unless we find more cash, this won't last."

From behind the brothers, Nat spoke up. "They're all dead right?"

"Yep," Judas nodded.

"We could make a bomb, take them all out at once."

Judas's eyes raised, "Now you're talking! How can we do that?"

"The science class is right over there." She pointed down the hall. "They've got everything we'd need."

Judas and Jonah shared a glance, and Jonah shrugged. "Why not? The chairs are keeping them in place. If they get through, it should only be a couple at a time. We just need to be quick."

The large heavyset zombie had made her way back onto her

feet and lumbered toward Jonah. Judas stepped in behind her, pulled out the scissors, grabbed her head back and slammed them into her temple. Green bile drained out, rushing down her neck and soaking her shirt, causing Judas to let go and jump back as the body fell. Liquid goo spread across the ground.

"C'mon," Jonah said, "don't step in that Nat, it's toxic."

The trio ran to the door marked 'Science'.

Behind them, the remaining zombies thrashed amongst the tangle of chairs, their growls echoing throughout the quiet hallway.

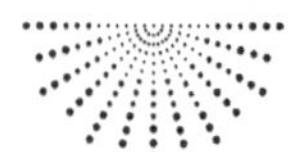

WHEN THEY ARRIVED at the door, they found it locked.

"Should've realized that was gonna happen. Lockdown." Jonah shook his head.

They all looked back down the hall; a lone zombie had made his way around the chairs and headed in their direction.

"What do you think Jonah, keep trying to take them out one at a time?"

"Can't," Jonah held up the pencil. "We can't reuse the weapons, they're toxic and it's getting worse. You saw how much that last one oozed out. Hopefully, the lunch lady comes back soon. In the meantime, trying to make a bomb is our best option."

Jonah peered through the small window in the door. There weren't any kids in the room, that was good. He reached down to where Brutus would normally be holstered, prepared to blast the lock off, only to have his hand swish through empty air. "Dammit," Jonah cursed in Judas's direction, then took a step back and slammed his foot against the door.

It shook, rattling nearby lockers as well, but didn't open. Two more kicks and the lock splintered. Jonah stepped back, winded and motioned to Judas. "Give it a go, bro."

Judas stepped up and landed a solid blow right next to the knob. The jam splintered and the deadbolt burst through the wood.

"Quick, inside," Jonah motioned, glancing at the approaching zombie. "Let this one go by for the moment until we've got options."

The three of them hustled into the science classroom and closed the door as best they could. Jonah knelt and held the bottom of the door to keep it closed.

"You two get started. I'll keep an eye on things out here."

The lone zombie arrived at the door and pawed at it, groaning. Jonah pushed against it, holding him back, the sharpened novelty pencil at the ready.

Judas turned to Nat. "What've you got in mind?"

"We've got all the chemicals necessary to create a gaseous mixture, and that, when combined and kept under pressure along with some sort of projectiles, will work like a grenade. It should pulverize them."

"Ok," Judas nodded. "I love science! It was the one subject I was ok at in school. What do we need?"

"Over in that closet," she pointed, "there's a box of beads. Get those, I'll get a cylinder we can use."

"Hey, you can't be in here!" a voice shouted in the hallway.

The zombie growled and turned from the door.

"That sounds like Mr. Simmons," Nat said. "He's my computer teacher."

"You mean the one that was flushing the fish with the other kids from your class?" Judas asked.

"Yes," Nat nodded. "The bathrooms don't have doors on them."

Jonah shot up and looked at Judas, who stopped before the supply closet. "You got this?"

Judas nodded. "Green and good to go. You go save those kids, we'll get this bomb made. When it's ready, we'll signal you somehow."

Jonah opened the door and poked his head out. The hungry corpse shambled toward Mr. Simmons, a short man with balding black hair. In the opposite direction, three more of the dead had made their way around the chairs and were coming to join the party. The light from the large glass window that ran along one side of the hall illuminated their blood stained clothes.

Jonah stepped out into the hall, sharpened pencil at the ready.

The teacher yelled at the approaching zombie and walked toward him. "You're not allowed in the school. You need to leave now."

"Stay away from him!" Jonah shouted.

Mr. Simmons stopped a few feet away from the zombie and looked at Jonah, his eyes widened even more, like suddenly he didn't know who he should be yelling at; the disheveled and grungy looking Jonah, or the bloody corpse that was almost on top of him.

Jonah ran toward them. "Get back!"

Mr. Simmons stood frozen, only taking a single step backward as the hungry and dead man lunged onto him. They collapsed onto the ground in a growling, screaming heap. Jonah ran up behind them, grabbed the zombie by the hair, and yanked his head away from the teacher. Seeing from the rush of red blood spraying out that he was too late for Mr. Simmons, he rammed the giant pencil through the creature's eye and shoved the body to the side.

A chorus of children's screams brought his attention to the bathroom, a few feet away. In the opening, two young girls and a boy stood, others behind them. They had watched as Jonah killed the zombie and now as he stood over the bleeding to death Mr. Simmons.

"Get back inside," Jonah shouted at them. "It's not safe out here."

"What is that thing?" the dying teacher asked him.

"A zombie," Jonah said, looking back at the others making their way down the hall.

"A zombie?" the man asked, his hands finding their way to the gaping hole in his neck. "How?" then, "oh God, he bit me! Does that mean... like on the TV shows?" He reached up, clutching Jonah's arm.

Jonah looked back at him. "I don't know how, but yeah, their bites are fatal."

The man's eyes trembled and he let go of Jonah's arm to clutch at the bite.

"How many kids are in the bathroom?"

Mr. Simmons blinked. "Uh, ten. No, nine. Nat stayed in the computer lab."

"Is there any way to lock it or close it off?"

"No," he shook his head. "It's just a large hallway that leads to the stalls and sinks." He paused as he struggled to sit up, staring down the hall to where more of the walking dead had passed the chairs. "How long do I have?"

"A few minutes usually." Jonah eyed the approaching ghouls, calculating.

The teacher's mouth moved, repeating Jonah's words. Then, stuck on one of them, repeating it three times before looking at Jonah, he asked, "Usually? What do you mean usually? Who are you?"

A loud metal rattling sounded from the other side of the hall. Jonah turned to see the large lunch lady rounding a corner, pushing a rickety metal cart. A catalogs worth of kitchen implements filled the shelves and on top, sat a large pink bag of what looked like silly putty, hanging over the sides.

"My name's Jonah Zee, sir. I'm a zombie exterminator."

The teacher nodded and offered a hand. "Could you help me up, Mr. Zee?"

Jonah grabbed his hand and pulled him to his feet. "Just Jonah's fine. My father was the only Mr. Zee I've ever known and I'm not sure I'll ever feel I've earned that title for myself."

Nurse Janet came rattling up behind them. The cart she had brought with her carried rolling pins, knives and a cleaver on the middle shelf and the giant plastic bag filled with white and pink goo on top. Jonah stopped short when he saw the logo on the side of the bag. It was two N's intertwined with one another, inside a circle.

"What is that?" he asked her.

"It's called pink slime. It's an additive we add to the lunch meat, helps keep costs down. It's mostly a meat byproduct. I thought since these things eat flesh it might be a good distraction."

"That logo though," Jonah pointed at it. "Aren't they a chemical manufacturer?"

"What?" Nurse Janet wrinkled her nose. "You think our food comes straight from farms anymore? It all goes through the corporations first. Most schools receive deliveries directly from the fast food chains these days. We tried to get away from that but the only option was to buy our own ingredients." She stopped as Mr. Simmons swayed on his feet beside her. She took in the sight of him. "Oh no!"

"There's kids in the bathroom." Jonah indicated toward the opening.

Janet walked over and glanced in, then shook her head. "This isn't going well. What's next, Mr. Exterminator? And where's the other one?"

"He's in the science lab making a bomb. We need to buy some ti—"

"A bomb?" Janet shouted. "Are you crazy? This is a school filled with children!"

Jonah backed away, raising his hands. "I know, I know. We don't have a lot to work with right now."

Nurse Janet stepped in front of him, waving her rolling pin menacingly. "I can't believe you'd—"

"Whoa, whoa," Jonah pushed his arms higher. "Put Lucille down lady, I'm doing the best I can."

Beside them, Mr. Simmons grabbed the metal cart by the railing and charged with a yell down the hall toward the approaching dead. Implements flew off the cart in every direction, creating a clamor as it bounced down the hall.

"Ahh!"

"What is he doing?" Nurse Janet asked.

"Buying us some time, I think. He was bitten."

"But the knives are on the cart."

"I know." Jonah shook his head. "Welcome to my world."

The cart slammed into the first corpse, knocking the dead man over. A thunderous clang pierced the air as the impact sent the pile of knives and remaining implements scattering across the floor. The giant bag of pink slime spilled out like an elephant vomiting. Mr. Simmons fell to the ground, weeping and sobbing as the dead reached him and lunged, completely ignoring the pile of processed meat product.

Janet watched a moment, then shook her head. "Not surprised. The rats don't even touch that stuff." She turned to face Jonah. "What do we do now?"

He ran over and picked up a large meat cleaver lying on the ground nearest them. "We need to keep these kids safe and get them outta here until we can take care of the dead." He indicated with a nod of his head the feasting trio and the others further down the hall who were mostly through the obstacle course of chairs. "Here they come."

PART X - WEIRD SCIENCE

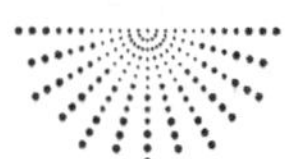

JUDAS PULLED out the heavy box marked 'Beads' and brought it over to the table Nantucket was working at. The box weighed at least thirty pounds. He opened the lid and blinked at what he saw.

"Um, Nat. These aren't glass beads." Judas scratched at his chin. "They're eyeballs. A whole box of 'em."

"I know," she said, adjusting the knob on a burner. "That's what we got sent, fake eyeballs. The school supply warehouse wouldn't take them back. So that's what we use. Mr. Gibbs always says a good scientist has to utilize the resources at hand."

Judas looked at the eyeballs, many of which stared back at him, and nodded. "Ok, fuck it. Nantucket, let's MacGyver this shit. What's next?" He laughed. "That would make a better nickname for you. Fuck-it Nantucket! How'd you end up with the name Nantucket, anyway?"

She pushed her glasses up on the bridge of her nose and tilted her head at him.

"Sorry," he said. "Didn't mean to offend you."

"Here," Nat shoved a two-foot tall and four-inch wide metal tube across to him. "Fill this."

Judas poured handfuls of glass eyeballs into the metal container, creating a cacophony of noise until it was full. He watched as Nantucket flipped through a notebook she'd removed from her backpack.

She stopped on a page and scanned through a series of hand-written notes, stopping on a section she had starred and put in a box. She'd also drawn a large letter B above it. She grabbed a metal measuring cup and opened a tub from under the table marked Sulfur, then scooped up half a cup, double checked her notes and poured it into the cylinder.

"Shake that so it settles to the bottom," she told Judas. "And you didn't offend me. I've been called a lot of names at this school; words are just words when they're said to me. It's when they're said to others about me that it's upsetting. I don't know what my parents were thinking. Well, I do. They met there on summer vacation one year, it's always been special to them and that makes sense. Naming me after the place... not so much."

Judas nodded and shook the container, his nose twitching from the smell, a smile formed on his face. "I've missed that scent."

"What do you mean?" Nat glanced up from measuring another powdered substance.

Judas stuck his tongue into his lip, searching for the tobacco he normally kept there. Not finding it, he tried the other side of his mouth, then remembered he didn't have any. He searched his pockets for more of the hard candies and spoke distractedly. "I used to make stink bombs with it all the time. I'd make these contraptions with a balloon that took about ten minutes to fill up with gas and then explode. I'd roll them under people's cars when they were making out." He grinned.

Nat looked at him and laughed. "That's horrible!"

"I know." Judas pulled out the package of peanut butter cups and the little tubular package of powder marked Energy-Os and looked at them. "I even did it to my brother once."

"What, why?"

"He took out a girl I had a crush on." Judas's mouth watered looking at the peanut butter and chocolate candy, but he put them back in his coat. They were for JJ. He tore open the foil tube of Energy-Os instead. "What is this stuff, anyway?"

Nat stopped measuring and looked at the tube Judas held. "Energy-Os? You've never had them before?"

"No. Never seen 'em."

"Then I wouldn't eat it, or if you do, only have a little. It's full of chemicals they feed us kids to keep us alert and attentive so that we get better grades. It's to make sure we rank high in the educational scoreboards. Which, of course, means more money for the school."

"Hmm," Judas tried to read the small printed list of ingredients on the package, squinted, sighed and poured the whole container in his mouth.

An instantaneous rush of elation flooded his system as the crystalline powder melted on his tongue. The sweet flavor sent tingles across his taste buds and created a gush of saliva. He swallowed it and grinned as the warm tingling sensation flowed from his tongue, down his throat and into his stomach. "That was like drinking cotton candy whiskey!"

Nantucket shook her head and turned back to her notes.

Judas's eyes focused on the paper, seeing the list she was working from. He scrunched up his eyebrows, thinking back to his time making stink bombs as a teenager. "My dad taught me how to make the stink bombs. Where'd you learn how to make something like this?"

Nat glanced up, saw him looking at the page she was working from and set the measuring cup on top of her notes. "I, um, read about it on the internet."

"Hmm," Judas nodded, sniffed loudly and fidgeted back and forth. "But why were you looking up how to make a bomb? Have you been radicalized?"

Nat pushed at the measuring cup with a finger as her cheeks flushed.

Judas studied her, then looked at the large metal tube on the table before them. "This is a pretty big bomb we're making. It's almost like you were ready to do this."

She chewed on the inside of her cheek and stared fixedly at the table.

Judas's mind was in full gallop. He tingled from head to toe and his thoughts were clearer then they'd ever been in his life. "What is it, Nat?"

A lone crocodile tear ran down her cheek. "I..." she fumbled over her words. "I hate this place." She stopped there and pushed the measuring cup around a little more.

"Why do you hate this place?" Judas knelt so that he was at eye level with her.

Nat lifted her eyes from the paper for a moment, looked in Judas's, then darted away.

"C'mon on Nat, we're fighting zombies together. Tell me what's going on?"

She looked back at him. "They don't really call me Nat the Nerd, well not anymore, they call me Nasty Natty."

"What?" Judas's eyes widened as he looked across at the young girl.

She tugged on one of the braided strands of dark hair and blinked through the wetness around her eyes. "They didn't like me much to begin with, being a black girl in a state where they dislike anyone a shade darker than tan. I started my period in class one day, and it bled right through my white pants. I didn't know what it was. There's this boy, Nick, I call him Nick the Dick and, at the end of class we all stood up, he saw it, pointed and laughed, calling me nasty. He got a bunch of other kids to join in and they started chanting Nasty Natty."

"That's awful." Judas reached out a hand and set it on top of hers. "And you were gonna blow them up?"

Nantucket sniffed, her nose running. "No, I wanted to. I wrote down the ingredients and even took notes on what I could use. It made me feel good knowing I *could* do it but I knew it was a bad idea. When I'm not at school, I have a good life."

Judas nodded and smiled at the girl. "Thank you for sharing that with me Nat. Bullies suck. Is that why you didn't go to the bathroom with the other kids?"

She nodded. "Yeah. Nick is in my computer class. He only wanted to go so he could watch 'Q' get flushed. I couldn't stand to listen to him, so I stayed behind."

Motion from outside the door caught Judas's attention. He glanced up, seeing two more of the dead walk by in the direction Jonah had gone. "Well, after today," he grinned at her and grabbed hold of the metal cylinder. "People will know you as Fuck-It Nantucket, the Zombie Slayer! What do we need to do next?"

Nat grinned back, lifted the measuring cup from her notes and found the next ingredient on her list. She turned around and grabbed a jug off a shelf.

Judas's body took on a mind of its own. He found his feet shifting back and forth and his teeth grinding together. He could hear the blood rushing through his veins. His desire for tobacco hadn't lessened, if anything the Energy-O's had made it worse.

"Mr. Judas?" Nat asked.

"Yeah?" Judas asked, moving his tongue around inside his mouth. It felt strange like it was no longer attached. He kept rubbing it against his teeth to make sure he could still control it.

"Energy-O's kicking in?"

"Yeah, I think so." He took his hat off and ran a hand through his hair. Every follicle buzzed. "This stuff is crazy." He stuck his tongue out, panting. "Ugh." He bent over and clutched his stomach. "It feels like I've been punched in the gut."

"Yeah, the first time's like that, especially if you take too much." Nat watched Judas a moment while continuing to pour liquid from the jug. "How did you and Mr. Jonah become zombie exterminators anyway?"

Judas, still bent over, answered. "We were just regular exterminators at first. We got a job with a company called Pests B' Gone. Worked for them a few months, got fired because of a co-worker and then found ourselves looking for work on Craigslist. We came across an ad for a corporation that was hiring for security work."

"Which one?" she asked, grabbing a beaker from a table behind her and filling it with water.

Judas blinked, eyes watering, stomach cramping and his tongue throbbing. "Huh?"

"Here, drink this. It should help."

Judas took the water and gulped it down.

"Which corporation?"

"Nitsau."

Nat nodded. "I've read about them on the internet. They're one of the shadow corporations behind the crisis that led to the U.C.A. being formed and taking over the country. They call them the Legion of Doom. Of course, everyone knew they owned the politicians anyway, the U.C.A. just made it official."

Judas set the empty beaker on the table and burped. "Oh." He blinked again and shook his head. "That's a bit better." He could feel his heart pounding in his chest, the blood racing in his veins, but his mind seemed clear.

"We were hired to work security for one of their research and production facilities outside of Tucson." Judas's words came out faster and faster as the rush of the Energy-O's hit him. "We ended up working for the CEO, Dr. Nitsau, a research physicist. She was doing experiments and, one day while we were on shift, they got out of control." His left eye twitched, his vision blurring, they itched terribly and he blinked and rubbed at them.

Nat stopped what she was doing and looked at Judas. "Zombie experiments?"

"Yeah," Judas shook his head and spun around in a circle. "I've got too much energy." He hopped up and down, waving his arms about.

She watched him a moment before returning to her notes. "We're almost ready. Why don't you go check the door and see what's happening."

"Good idea," Judas bounded across the room, looked out the door and sprinted back. "They're through the chairs and spread out all over the hallway. I don't see Jonah. He's probably with the kids in the bathroom. There's a cart filled with hamburger or something sitting there that they're ignoring. How much longer? Are you done? What do you need?"

"Almost," Nat said. "I've got a few more ingredients to add, then the chemical reaction will start. We'll need to screw that lid on the end of the cylinder, and that'll leave us approximately one minute before it explodes."

"Ok. What do I do?" Judas bounced on his toes. "This stuff is driving me bonkers. You kids eat this every day?"

"Most do," she gave a bitter smile. "It's almost mandatory. If you're on any kind of assistance program, it's included in your free meals. Helps give people a leg up, they say."

Judas frowned. "They force kids to take this stuff?"

"Yep," Nantucket nodded. "It's all in the name of a better education."

"That's crazy! This stuff is stronger than cocaine!" Judas's head fluttered around as he spoke.

"Well, you really shouldn't have eaten the whole packet. The way most kids get it, it's only a little bit at a time, keeps them alert and attentive."

Judas seemed to drift far away, his eyes losing focus until Nat's voice brought him back to his body.

"Mr. Judas!" the girl yelled.

"Yeah, what is it, kid?" Judas shook his head and wiped sweat from his brow.

"What happened when the experiment got out of control?"

"Oh, um," Judas squinted at her, moving his eyes around, trying to get focused. "We, uh, we were gate security at the time. Checking vehicles in and out of the facility, that kind of thing. One day, there were screams coming from inside, so we went in, these creatures, zombies, were everywhere, feasting on lab techs and civilians. We were right next to the emergency fire kit. Jonah grabbed the axe and I grabbed the extinguisher. I'd blast them in the face to distract them and he'd put the axe in their head. We didn't know what they were at first, or how to stop them, we just started hacking."

"Wow," Nat stared at him, holding her hand to her throat as she listened.

"When it was over, Dr. Nitsau came out of a safe room in the back of the lab and offered us jobs as her personal security. From there, we were given equipment and training and did whatever was asked of us." Judas trailed off, either spacing out again or uncertain how to continue.

"So, you still work for them?"

Judas shook his head. "No, no." He stopped to groan and clutch at his stomach again. Beads of sweat dripped from his forehead. "We, uh, left the doctor's employment after an incident that didn't end well, and went out on our own. Turns out there's plenty of random outbreaks happening all the time. All we had to do was apply for a permit from the U.C.A. and keep up our paperwork."

"I always thought they were made up to scare people."

"Nope. We learned all sorts of different ways the dead can come back to life. Viruses, curses, neurotoxic gas, parasites, genetic modification, the list goes on and on. The doctor had a team of scientists studying them."

"Wow, what for?"

Judas looked away, his head twitching as he bounced on the balls of his feet. He looked back and forth from the door to the bomb. One hand clutched at his stomach, the other at his chest. "Kid, I don't feel too good. Is that bomb ready yet?"

INSIDE THE BATHROOM, eight kids, three girls and five boys of various ages, most crying, huddled in a corner by the stalls. All except one, a tall and lanky boy wearing brown khaki pants and a tan hoodie, who stood apart from them, head down, arms crossed.

Jonah came in first and all eyes looked up at him. Two of the girls burst into fresh tears. The boy standing alone looked him over, examining his worn and dirty clothes, eyes widening at the sight of the cleaver. "Who are you? Where's Mr. Simmons?"

"I'm a professional," Jonah said, looking over his shoulder for Janet. "We're here to help."

The lunch lady came in next, her rolling pin in one hand, a knife in the other.

The boy took her in, then spun back to Jonah. "A professional what? The school's on lockdown and they send in the gardener and the lunch lady to save us?"

Jonah stopped short; *What the hell was up with this kid?* "No, I'm a zombie exterminator."

"A what? Those aren't real."

"Look kid, what's your name?"

"Nick."

"My name's Jonah, and right now, we need to get you and your classmates out of here. They're coming."

Jonah scanned the small room. A series of small rectangular windows ran above the stalls in the back. They looked like they opened, but they weren't very big.

"I don't believe you," Nick said.

Jonah shook his head. "I don't care. Shut up and do what you're told."

"You can't talk to me like that. I'll call my parents and they'll call Mr. Hotchkins."

Jonah threw his hands in the air. "Go ahead, kid. Mr. Hotchkins is one of them."

This brought cries from the younger kids.

"Shit, sorry. Look, we need to—"

A moan from the doorway behind them grabbed their attention. Jonah and Janet spun. A bloody-faced middle-aged man lumbered in and moved to attack Janet.

"Kids," Jonah shouted, "get in the stalls. Close the doors and stand on the toilets."

Janet clunked the body over the head with her rolling pin, knocking it back, but not stopping it.

"You're either going to need to pound it like your name is Neegan or use the knife," Jonah said from behind her. "You have to destroy the brain. That's how ninety-nine percent of zombies work. But with these, they're poisonous too, so make sure not to get any blood or green goo on you if you can help it."

Janet looked at the rolling pin which now had red muck all over it from the zombie's massacred face. "This isn't easy, is it?"

"No ma'am, it really isn't."

She eyed the approaching gore-covered corpse, holding the rolling pin in her right hand and the knife in her left. She switched implements from one hand to the other. The zombie reached for her. She hefted the rolling pin and swung her meaty arm in an outward arc, connecting with the zombie's head and sending it sprawling to the ground. "Fuckwit."

Before it could recover, she was on it and rammed the knife under its chin, through the throat and into the brain. The zombie grunted and went still. Blood oozed from the wound as Janet slid it back out.

"Ugh, that smells like hell." The knife dripped a stream of red blood tinged green.

"Don't let that get on you!" Jonah shouted. "Rinse that knife off in the sink. You're going to need it again."

"What is it?" she asked, glancing at him as she turned the faucet on. "What's causing this?"

Jonah felt around in his pockets as he replied. "I don't know where it's coming from, but it's a poisonous gas, some sort of nerve toxin. Leftovers from a government experiment more than likely. It turns people into radioactive zombies. Their bites and bodily fluids can infect others."

"Oh no."

"Yeah, it's nasty stuff. It seems like it might've started with the principal, but I've no idea how he could've gotten infected. The longer they're undead, the more toxic they get." He smiled as his fingers found the cylindrical package he was hoping to find in an internal jacket pocket. He pulled out a half-smoked cigar and stuck it in his mouth. It was dry and brittle, but when you might die in the next few minutes, any cigar was a good cigar.

Janet shook water from the blade and wiped it on her apron. "No. It started with a boy. His name's Tommy Tucker. He came to school sick."

"That means it started somewhere else." Jonah shook his head. "This could get a whole lot worse." Moans from out in the hall stopped him short. He whispered, "We need to get these kids out of here."

Janet nodded and stepped away from the entry.

"I'll get one of those windows open and we can lift the kids up and through it, then I'll help you out." Jonah set the cleaver on top of a sink.

Janet looked at the small windows then back at Jonah. "I'm not the kind of woman who climbs out of windows. I'm a woman of a certain stature." She stood straighter, tugging the chef's apron she wore over her belly. "Just get the kids to safety."

Jonah glanced at the windows. "Ok, I'm not sure I'd fit through either."

The kids had crowded into the three stalls. The girls in the far left, the four younger boys in the middle and Nick in the last by himself. Jonah went to the girls. Opening the door elicited a small scream from one and a series of questions from another.

A thin girl with pale skin and short dark hair cut into a bob looked up at him from atop the toilet. "Are we going to get eaten?"

"No," Jonah said. "We're gonna get you out that window to safety."

"But those things want to eat us." This caused the other girl to start crying.

From two stalls over, Nick commented, "You little cry-babies."

Jonah bit his tongue, looking at the two crying children. He reached out to touch one of them, then stopped as the eyes of the talkative one saw his missing fingers and he pulled it away before the others noticed it.

The little dark-haired girl stared at him. "Did they do that?"

Jonah shook his head. "No, not them. That happened a while ago."

"Did it hurt?"

"Yes. Now—"

A loud groan came from right outside the bathroom. The girls cried out and Jonah turned to see shadowy shapes moving around the entrance. Nurse Janet stood a few feet away, facing the door, rolling pin and knife at the ready.

"Ok girls," Jonah said, reaching out. "I need you to move so I can get up there and open that window." He pointed at it. "We're gonna get you out of here."

The inquisitive girl stepped down and offered her hand to help a blond girl that was the same height as her. The last girl trembled, tears streaming.

"Mr. Jonah. I'm too scared."

"I know you are," Jonah said. Looking around, he tried to figure out some way to calm her. Spying a hair pin in her hair with a little poodle on it, he found inspiration. "Do you like dogs?"

"Wh-what?" The girl asked him through her tears.

"Do you like dogs? I see you have one in your hair."

She sniffed her runny nose and looked at him with a wrinkled forehead. "Why?"

"There's a really cute dog coming. He'll be outside in just a little bit. You'll get to meet him."

The dark haired girl tugged on Jonah's pant leg. "It's not a zombie dog is it?"

"No," Jonah shook his head. "We didn't bring the zombies, we're here to get rid of them."

The crying girl moved out of his way and he stepped onto the toilet, reached up and flipped the latch on the window.

"What's his name?" the scared, crying girl asked.

"Xanadu."

PART XII - ZOMBIE SWIRLY

THE SLEEK, charcoal gray Charger screeched to a stop behind the brothers' red Prius in front of Savini Charter School. JJ had one hand on the wheel and the other keeping Xanadu from flying out of his seat.

"Where the hell are the cops?" She scooped Xanadu under one arm and hopped out her door. "C'mon boy, were probably going to need you."

She set him on the ground and ran over to the brothers' car. Finding it locked, she turned back to her own and popped the trunk. She had her revolver strapped to her hip, a knife on her belt; what else was back here she could use? The trunk resembled the dumpster outside a thrift store donation center. Clothes, books, bags of stuff were everywhere.

She shoved the debris aside, revealing a black leather satchel stuffed into the left corner. A small cardboard box marked 'Xanadu Droppings' was behind it with an even smaller wrapped box beside that. *I've got to remember to grab the baggy out of the glove box and put it in there,* she reminded herself. She reached for the satchel and saw the handle of a riding crop and a pair of black vinyl panties sticking out of the zippered opening. "That's not going to help now is it..." She shook her head.

She spied something that caught her eye: a bright orange, v-necked t-shirt, with two dark brown shapes across the front. "Oh, I've been looking for that. They'll love it." She slipped her leather jacket off, glanced around to see if anyone was about - it was eerily quiet - then peeled her tank top off, tossing it in the trunk and yanking the vintage t-shirt over her shoulders. The pair of large peanut butter cups, with the slogan, 'Two of your favorite things' underneath it, lined up perfectly with her breasts. Her smile widened as she slid her coat back on.

Underneath where the shirt had been, she found a rusted crowbar. "This'll work." She grabbed it, closed her trunk and ran for the front door of the school. At the top of the stairs, she found Judas's knife. "What the hell is this doing out here?"

JJ picked it up and slid it in her belt. "I bet he'll want this back."

She pulled on the door handle and found it locked. Looking through the window she saw the metal barricade behind it and cursed. "No way I'm getting through that." She pounded on the door to see if anyone would come and peered through the grates at the bloody debris in the hallway.

After a moment, a form came around the corner inside. It was a woman, her mouth, and throat covered in red, her white blouse torn open, exposing a pair of large blood stained breasts. Despite the fact the woman was dead, JJ felt a twinge of jealousy as she looked at the woman's blood-covered tits.

"That better not be Jonah or Judas's," she growled. The woman slammed into the barricade. "I'm gonna need to find another way in. C'mon boy!" She took off at a jog, following the outline of the school, Xanadu at her heels, his new bandana flapping in the breeze.

IN THE BATHROOM, Jonah lifted Emily, the short dark haired girl to the window, as he balanced himself, being careful his foot didn't slip into the open toilet bowl. "Just drop to the ground on the other side and go climb the tallest piece of playground equipment until help arrives."

"Ok, Mr. Jonah," the girl said. "Thank you for being so brave."

Jonah smiled.

"I can't wait to meet your dog Xanadu." She climbed through the small window.

Jonah opened his mouth to say it wasn't his dog when a loud growl came from the entrance. He spun and watched as the lunch lady sunk her knife into the head of another PTA member. Green rushed out, covering the knife, some of it spraying on Janet's apron.

"Get back," Jonah shouted. "Let go of the knife." He stepped off the toilet and ran up behind her. "Remember, that green stuff is poison. Don't let it get on your skin."

"Ok," she nodded, "but what are we gonna do? We don't have enough weapons to fend off very many." She picked the cleaver up off the sink.

"Let's hope Judas and Nat get that bomb made quick!"

"Do you really think that's a good idea?"

"No, but right now, I ain't got a better one."

Jonah turned to go help the boys out the next window when Janet let out a cry. Turning back, he saw four more hungering dead looking for some of that lunch lady special. "Shit! Get in the empty stall!" he shouted at her. "Close the door and make them come to you. If they come under it, either bash their heads in or stomp on 'em if you have to. I'll get these boys out of here."

He opened the stall door and squeezed in with the four young boys huddled there. From the stall next to them, Nick cried out, "Hey, what about me?"

"I'll get to you next. Just lock your stall door and stay off the ground."

The first zombie smashed into Jonah's door causing the remaining children to shriek as the stalls rattled.

Jonah hefted the first boy to the window. "Go-go!"

From Janet's stall he heard a loud creaking, she cried out. "Oh shit! The lock's broken."

A moment later cries rang out from Nick's stall. "They're coming under!"

The first lunch bell sounded.

IN THE SCIENCE LAB, Judas paced the floor, his tongue repeatedly probing the empty space in his lip for tobacco that wasn't there. His hands absentmindedly searched his pockets for more of the hard candies, ending with the peanut butter cups which he considered for a moment. "No, those are for JJ. Gotta save those for JJ," he said to himself.

This same, absent minded frenzied behavior looped over and over until Nat interrupted him.

"Mr. Judas?"

Judas stopped, turned to the kid and blinked, shook his head a few times, stuck his tongue out and said, "Yeah?"

"The bomb's ready."

Judas parroted what she had said, the words at first empty of meaning. "The bomb's ready?" He tilted his head and stared at her, "The bomb's ready?" Then, at least temporarily, he snapped out of his chemically induced daze. "The bomb's ready!" He rushed over to the counter where Nat stood. The large metal tube stood upright between them, with the end cap off and a beaker of liquid waiting next to it.

"All we need to do is add this," she raised the beaker, "and screw the lid on. The chemical reaction will start immediately."

"How long will it take?" Judas's head vibrated back and forth as he spoke.

"Thirty seconds to two minutes. The casing will swell and then," Nat made exploding sounds and threw her hands into the air. "Scrambled Zombies!"

"At least it's not an omelet this time."

Nat's brow furrowed. "Are you okay Mr. Judas?"

"Yeah," Judas twitched. "Don't do drugs. Those Energy-O's are messed up."

"I told you, you shouldn't eat the whole packet."

He stopped moving a moment and looked at her. There was a silence in which Judas's stomach gurgled so loud, they both looked down at it. He shook his head. "Look, I'm as green as I'm gonna be." He turned and ran to the door. "Shit, they're all bunched up by the bathroom." He ran back. "We can't explode it right there. I'm gonna have to get their attention and lead them back down the hall."

"Ok, what do we do?"

"You hide." Judas grabbed the beaker of liquid and poured it into the open cylinder. It hissed and a puff of chemical smoke rose from the top. He grabbed the lid, spun it on and twisted it tight. "I'm gonna run really fast." He swooped the heavy cylinder under his arm and bolted for the door.

The first lunch bell rang.

❋

"HOLD 'EM OFF!" Jonah shouted to Janet over the ringing of the lunch bell. "Use that cleaver." He glanced over the top of the stall to where Nick screamed from his precarious position on the toilet seat. "Stomp on 'em if you have to, kid. I'll help as soon as I can."

Nick blubbered something back, his words a jumbled stuttering mess, his eyes wide and wet.

Jonah hoisted the second young boy up to the window, then reached down and grabbed the other two. Holding one in each arm, he pulled them up from the grasping hands coming under the stall. They cried out in both fear and relief. Beneath them, the toilet rocked and Jonah struggled to keep his feet from slipping off the porcelain edge.

He looked out into the restroom. There were eight to ten zombies in with them now, and more bunched at the door. Their hungry groans filled the air.

Janet pushed back against her door, keeping it from opening, but the dead were reaching around the edge, grasping at her. If she pushed too hard, she would end up right in their midst.

Jonah got his footing on top of the toilet seat and lifted another of the boys. "C'mon, out you go." He counted the seconds as he waited for the boy to scramble through the opening. "Could really use Xanadu right about now," he muttered under his breath and wished he had time to check if JJ had called.

Both Janet and Nick were screaming. He could see the bloody hands reaching under his stall and knew time was short. He got the last of the boys out through the window and turned to find Janet sinking the cleaver into a zombie's skull. Blood sprayed out, covering the wall next to her. Two more were pushing in right behind it, trampling their dead brother as they came to feast on the lunch lady.

Jonah pushed the soggy cigar from one side of his mouth to the other and turned to Nick's stall, noticing as he did so that the room had emptied out some, and the entryway to the bathroom stood clear.

Nick's horrified screams filled the air and Jonah leaned over the top. One of the dead had crawled under and was grasping the edge of the bowl, pulling itself inside. Nick huddled against the back wall, kicking his foot out like he was pushing over a dead animal to see if it was alive. His shoe tapped against the zombie's skull and then pulled away.

"C'mon kid," Jonah said, reaching out his arm. "Kick and let's go."

The boy looked up, terror painted on his face.

Despite the kid's earlier arrogance, Jonah felt sorry for him.

"C'mon, c'mon! Grab my hands!"

The boy stared at him, frozen until the creature's hand wrapped around his leg and a fresh scream ripped from Nick's lungs.

The zombie pulled and Nick slipped, one foot splashing into the bowl, the other flailing.

Jonah grabbed one of his wild, waving hands. "I've got you! Grab my other hand." He pulled on the boy as the zombie got hold of his leg and yanked in the other direction, bringing himself in for a bite.

"Mr. Erickson, no!" The boy cried.

Jonah grabbed the boys other hand and heaved, the zombie tug-of-war bringing both of them up.

The dead Mr. Erickson was halfway inside the stall now, his body contorted into an S. The dead man's mouth gaped open and it came up from beneath the boy, pulling himself up by Nick's pant leg.

The boy watched the gaping mouth come for him and screamed.

Jonah did the only thing he could think of. He let go.

OUT IN THE HALL, the mass of dead were pushing and shoving to get inside the bathroom. A few stragglers littered around back by the chair barricade. In the distance outside the large window, Judas could see a shape moving in his direction, he hoped they hadn't gotten outside the school. He shouted toward the bathroom, "Jonah, if you can hear me, the bomb's ready. Get somewhere safe!"

A few of the group turned, growling in Judas's direction. He spun around and saw the cafeteria cart with its ignored bag of meat product oozing off the top of it, smiled and said, "Perfect."

He ran over to it and shoved the cylinder in the middle of the pink mess, grabbed the cart handle and spun it around, the little wheels rattling like thunder.

"Come and get it," he yelled. "It's feeding time!"

The racket he made got their attention and more zombies poured from the bathroom and came for him. Judas glanced behind himself to make sure none of the stragglers were to close and started backing up.

"C'mon, you hungry buggers!"

They came, slowly. Certainly much slower than the frenzied pace at which Judas was moving. He belched as his stomach rumbled. The cylinder in front of him swelled. He shook the cart back and forth, making as much noise as possible.

The second lunch bell rang.

A pounding sounded on the large plexiglass window in the hall. He turned and JJ stood there, eyes wide.

"Judas!" her muffled voice shouted and she pointed behind him.

He whirled to find one of them was now almost on him. He twisted the cart around and bashed into it, knocking it over. He pivoted back to JJ and smiled. "Thank you!" he mouthed and pointed at the cylinder. "It's a bomb!"

The crowd of zombies grew nearer.

Her face scrunched in confusion as she shook her head, "Huh?"

"A bomb!" Judas pointed at it and threw his arms wide illustrating an explosion.

JJ nodded, mouthing back to him, "Bomb."

"Yes," Judas nodded, waving his arm at her to run. He shoved the cart toward the zombies. The cylinder on top of it bulged with hundreds of little bumps as the pressure inside built, pushing the beads into the metal.

JJ bent and came back up with Xanadu in her arms.

Judas yelled, "Throw him!" motioning with his arms as he turned and ran.

JJ ran parallel on the outside, guessing at how far to go before throwing her dog into the air and shouting his name.

"Xanadu!"

IN THE BATHROOM, Jonah couldn't hear the boy's scream over the second lunch bell as he fell. He only saw the panicked face as Nick cried out. His feet landing on top of the zombie's head and smashing it into the open toilet bowl.

Jonah dove over the top, his mid-section balancing him atop the stall wall and causing him to gasp, spitting his cigar to the floor.

The kid's shoes splashed in the water as he thrashed about, trying to escape the remains of Mr. Erickson. The zombie gurgled in the toilet water.

Jonah grabbed the boy's flailing arms and yanked, pulling him up and over, just as a familiar disco beat filled the air, followed by a slow building, 'Booooooooooom!'

PART XIII - EYEBALL BOMB

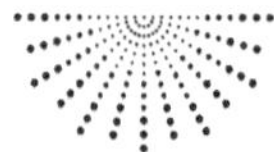

DUST. Chaos. Debris.

Jonah blinked.

The sound of a toilet flushing over and over again came from the remainder of the stall next to him. He remembered the music. *Xanadu? JJ?* A vague image of eyeballs shooting through the air flashed through his mind. *Judas. What?* The door lay atop him as did the boy he'd pulled from the other side. He shook his head to clear it and heard the moans of Janet, followed by the groans of the dead. "This job isn't done yet," he said and pushed the door away, struggling to get up. He slid Nick's unconscious form to the side and checked the boy's legs; no bites that he could tell. The haze of dust in the room kept visibility low, but from what he could hear, others were moving in the room. Water rushed from broken pipes and electricity crackled. All three bathroom stalls were in pieces.

"Miss?" Jonah crawled over the wreckage toward the lunch lady. "Are you okay? Can you hear me?"

"Grrrooowllll," the voice of a zombie rose from somewhere close.

Jonah's hand found the cleaver handle sticking out from a pile of debris, he grabbed it and stood on shaking legs. He stared into the surrounding haze. Something touched his boot, and he looked to find the partial remains of a zombie crawling across the floor, its intestines trailing behind it.

Thunk!

He sunk the cleaver into its head. Another groan sounded behind him and he spun.

"Are they dead?" the lunch lady asked in a raspy voice.

"Not quite," Jonah said, feeling around with his free hand. "They're in pieces though. Any that remain should be easy to deal with. But watch out for the green goo."

"And the kids?"

"Out the window, except the older one. He's okay though, no bites at least." Jonah knelt when he found the lunch lady's arm. "How about you?"

Janet coughed. "I'm okay, I think. They didn't get a piece of me."

Jonah flashed a smile that changed to a look of concern as he saw her face, grimacing in pain in the settling dust.

"I think maybe my arm's broken. It was the strangest thing, I was swinging the cleaver toward one of them and then it was like everything stopped. I watched the explosion happen. There were…," she shook her head. "There were eyeballs everywhere?"

"Yeah, I saw that too."

"And then," she continued, "the stall door broke away and knocked me back against the wall. I felt my arm snap, watched the cleaver fall and then it was now. What the hell was all of that?"

Jonah turned and surveyed the room. The pieces of half a dozen zombies littered the demolished restroom. He made a note of which ones were still moving. "I've no idea on the eyeballs, the rest, that was Xanadu." He pulled the cleaver from the head of the zombie he'd killed and moved to leave. "I need to go check on my brother. Will you tend to the boy?"

"Yes, but wait a sec," Janet said.

"Yeah?"

"What's a Xanadu?"

"A dog."

"A dog?" she shook her head, confused.

"Yep. I can't explain it either. Belongs to our girlfriend, JJ."

Janet nodded. "Jonah, I'm sorry I gave you so much grief earlier. You did a good job. You saved a lot of kids."

Jonah smiled and nodded at her. "Thank you. We couldn't have done it without you." He started away, stopping at each still moving corpse and sinking the cleaver into whatever looked like a head. Some were more obvious than others.

In the dusty hallway, light streamed through the large hole that had been ripped through the exterior wall. Chunks of concrete and ceiling tile lay strewn atop the bodies. Glass eyes were everywhere, rolling across the floor, embedded in walls and lockers.

Nantucket peered out from the remains of the science lab's door, taking it all in. Moans rose from the buried dead. Evidently blowing them to smithereens didn't quite do the trick after all. She let out a gasp when a torso atop the debris moved. One arm, its only arm, stretched up grasping into the air as its charred head twitched.

Then, stepping into the settling dust, a woman appeared, outlined from behind by the sun's spotlight. She wore tight blue jeans and a zipped up leather coat. Her long reddish-blond hair rested over her shoulders and she hefted a crowbar in her right hand. She swung it down and crushed the charred zombie's head like a melon.

A small dog with a black and orange bandana stepped in at her heels.

Nat grinned from ear to ear. "What a badass!"

The woman looked up, spied Nantucket standing in the tattered doorway and smiled. "Hi, my name's JJ," she said. "You happen to know where my friend Jonah is?"

"He's uh," Nat glanced up and down the hallway. "Mr. Jonah is in the bathroom."

"Mr. Jonah, huh?" she laughed. "I kinda like that. Been thinking about calling him Sir myself. Thanks, sweetie."

JJ stepped further into the damaged hallway, sinking the end of the crowbar into another undead head. When she pulled it out, it dripped green and red. She leaned in and peered at it.

"Don't touch that," Jonah's voice boomed.

"Ah!" JJ jumped and Xanadu barked. "You scared me!"

"Sorry, JJ. That stuff's toxic. It can turn you!"

She looked around the destroyed hallway where body parts were strewn and oozed the bloody green mixture. "It's everywhere."

"I know," Jonah said, taking it in. "We had to improvise. Things got out of control fast."

"Out!" JJ turned to Xanadu and pointed toward the grass.

He looked at her, lowered his head and slunk back outside.

Jonah stepped atop the debris holding his t-shirt over his face. "It's probably best we don't breathe this stuff in. Cover your mouth with something."

JJ looked around a moment, pursing her lips, set the crowbar down and unzipped her jacket, revealing the bright orange shirt with its chocolate peanut butter cups emblazoned across it. She paused as she slipped her jacket off to look at Jonah, making sure he was looking, then across the hall to the girl. "Better close your eyes, honey."

The shirt didn't hide much, but when JJ reached down and grabbed the bottom of it, Nat's eyes popped wide open, then she rushed to cover them with her hands.

Jonah smiled but shook his head. "I can't believe you go out like that."

"What?" she said, peeling the tight top over her head, exposing her large breasts to him. "I didn't buy 'em to hide 'em. My mother always said our mammies are natural and we shouldn't be ashamed of them."

Jonah's cheeks burned as he watched her. "You just said you bought them?"

"Yep," she picked up her leather coat and slipped it back on. "First thing I bought myself with Xanadu's little surprises."

"Then that's not natural," Jonah said, and immediately bit his tongue.

JJ's hands fell away from the zipper she was about to pull up, leaving her breasts exposed as she glared at him. "Excuse me? Not natural? Just because I'm a C-cup now instead of the double-A I was born with doesn't make them any less natural."

Jonah stumbled over his words. "No, JJ, I meant, uh, crap. I don't know what I meant, just uh, haven't you ever heard of a bra?"

She stared at him, lips parting as her nostrils flared, his cheeks flushed brighter. JJ grabbed the bottoms of her coat and connected the zipper. Her breasts smashed between her arms as she pushed them together and pulled the zipper up while staring him down.

"Yes, I've heard of a bra, you oaf!" She inched the zipper upward, her cleavage getting tighter as it slowly disappeared. "I have quite a few. In fact, breast sizes can go up or down an entire cup size throughout the month depending on where a woman is in her menstrual cycle!"

Sweat beaded around Jonah's hairline and left trails on his dusty cheeks.

"So, obviously, the responsible thing to do is, hit the mall and buy cute bras on a regular basis." She reached the very top of her coat's zipper, fully covering not only her breasts but most of her neck as well.

On the grass behind her, Xanadu lay watching the scene, shaking his head.

Jonah opened his mouth to speak.

"No!" JJ stopped him. "I'm not done. The only reason I don't have one on now is because I went to your garage first thing this morning to say hi to you before taking Xanadu to the groomers. I wanted to flirt with you! I was going to the gym after the groomers, then back to my apartment. But now, I'm here! To help you!" She tugged the already zipped zipper. "There. They're put away. You don't have to worry about seeing my nipples or anything else now."

A cry sounded from down the hall toward the office.

JJ who was done, but wasn't done, added, "And the only reason I didn't have one on the night I met you was because I was taking my dog for a walk and going to bed afterward, so don't think I always run around like this. Though there's nothing wrong with being naked!"

Jonah ran a hand across his forehead, wiping the sweat away. "I'm sorry. That's not what I meant. I like them, I want to—"

"Where's the nice one?" JJ interrupted. "Where's Judas?" She turned away from Jonah and looked into the dark and dust-filled hallway Judas had run down.

Jonah followed her gaze as a shape crawled across the wreckage, emerging from the dust.

Judas, on his knees, his hat clutched in one hand, looked up at JJ. He muttered her name, smiling. "JJ." Then he doubled over, groaned, clutched his stomach and vomited.

She turned away, giving Jonah a quick glance and mouthing, "Again?" She turned back to Judas. "At least you got my name right that time, sugar." Then she screamed.

A shirtless woman, her own breasts exposed and her face covered in blood, lunged from the darkness, landing directly on top of Judas.

"No!" JJ and Jonah shouted in unison, both dropping the shirts that covered their faces and breaking into a run.

PART XIV - JUDAS LOVES BOBBIE

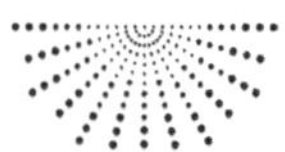

A HEARTBEAT before the bomb exploded, Judas reached the end of the hallway. He used the corner to hurtle himself into the darkness of the entry as the disco beat started. The force of his momentum and the power of the blast threw him forward. He slammed into a soft body in the darkness, his arms wrapping around it instinctively, and together they collided with the metal shutters that blocked the front doors of the school.

The ground shook and an eruption of noise rolled through the hallway behind him, drowning out the disco music. The zing of marble eyeballs whizzing through the air was followed by a thunderous crash as part of the ceiling collapsed. Dust and debris filled the air.

Judas panted for breath, his blood still racing and his stomach churning from the near-death experience, plus the chemical rush of the Energy-Os. His arms held the body in front of him. He moved his hands, recognizing the soft flesh of a woman's belly in one and a large breast in the other.

His mind exploded with a thousand thoughts. *Who is this? How did her shirt get torn open? That feels nice! I shouldn't be doing that. Do I smell blood? I feel sick.*

He pulled his hands away and stepped back. "I'm sorry miss, I didn't mean to... are you all right? I wasn't sure what was going on, the explosion..." His voice was a rush of words, fueled by the Energy-O's and the awkwardness of the moment. He pulled his shirt over his face as dust filled the air from the mayhem in the hall.

The woman turned and the first thing Judas saw was her chest. Her blouse stood wide open, torn down the middle, leaving both breasts exposed. He might not have looked anywhere else, but she lunged forward, causing him to step back, dropping his shirt from his face as he threw his hands up in apology.

"Miss, I'm sorry. I didn't mean—" He saw the scarlet stain on her throat, the red mask of caked blood on her chin, cheeks, and mouth, and then she was on top of him. Her breath washed over him, hot and stinking of iron.

"Oh shit!" He fell backward, arms jutting out to stop her as she rushed to take a bite out of his face. They fell, his hat flying off. He caught her right arm with his left and found his other hand once again on her breasts. Together they slammed into the tile floor, knocking the wind out of Judas.

He gasped for air with the dead woman grappling atop him, her breast jiggling in his hand and one of her nylon covered knees rubbing against his crotch. *Second base and heavy petting,* he thought as he pushed to keep her back, tearing off the little that remained of her blouse. *That's the farthest I've made it in a while.* He found himself strangely aroused as the woman thrust herself forward for a bite, grunting and growling inches from his face, then recognition clicked in.

"Bobbie?" he said, his voice shaking.

"Graaaar!" the dead woman responded, drool and blood running from her mouth in a pink trail.

Oh my God! Judas's mind raced. Bobbie Burns! His middle

school crush, in the flesh. He hadn't seen her in years. His hand squeezed tighter around the breast he had spent most of his puberty longing to touch. How many times had she come up to him with that cute little smile and pretended they'd never met? He'd always have something planned out to say, but she'd beat him to it. "Hi! I'm Bobbie, one Oh," then she'd push her arms in, squeezing her boobs together and say, "and two Bees." She'd laugh and walk away as Judas's young primal brain shut down, any chance of a witty response or even intelligible words lost.

Now, here she was on top of him, wanting him, her mouth gaped open and, for a fleeting moment, he wanted to kiss those hungry, bloody lips. Then he remembered in high school, she had asked Jonah on a date. He'd gone. Judas's blood boiled.

He'd shown them though. Making that stink bomb and rolling it under their car while they made out. The brothers hadn't talked for weeks after that, but Jonah had finally come to him and apologized, saying he should've known better, Judas had dibs, and thereafter they'd used that system whenever they met a new woman; one of them called dibs. Until JJ, that is. She was a different story altogether.

His eyes opened wider. *JJ! She was here! The bomb? Was she able to get out of the way?* He shoved Bobbie's body hard to the left, knocking her off him. He crawled to his feet, heard Bobbie groaning behind him and looked at a chunk of concrete debris laying next to his hat. For a moment, he considered picking it up and smashing the woman's head, but he glanced at her and that old childhood puppy love swelled; she was just too cute. Someone else would have to do that one.

He grabbed his hat and started away into the dusty chaos of the hallway. Light streamed in from holes everywhere and eyeballs littered the floor. He pulled his shirt up over his face again and groaned as the sick tightness in his stomach grew worse, his mouth watering as if he might throw up.

Ahead of Judas, most of a wall and part of the ceiling had

collapsed, creating a large pile of rubble on the ground. He could hear the moans of the dead beneath it. On the far side, he could see light. He clutched his stomach and told himself, he only had to get to the other side and he could relax. Check on JJ and Jonah and Nat and—

His eyes opened wide again. He groped around his body in a panic until his hand grasped the package of peanut butter cups. Still there!

Judas let out a momentary sigh of relief, before his stomach plummeted again, just like being on a roller coaster right as it dropped. He doubled over, fell to his knees and crawled forward over the wreckage until finally, like a goddess, he saw her standing in a halo of sunlight. He mouthed her name and vomited.

PART XV - BYE BYE BOBBIE

JONAH AND JJ ran toward Judas as he threw up, both screaming at him. He couldn't stop. Whatever chemicals they put in the Energy-O's, his body wanted them out. He felt the hands on his back as Bobbie lunged from the darkness for a piece of him. "Grrrr," he heard as her weight knocked him flat into his puke. He cried out and dropped his hat, the wind knocked out of him.

Then JJ & Jonah were there, ripping her off him and tossing her back into the debris. They knelt, turned him over, helped him sit up and checked him for bites.

"Were you bitten?" Jonah asked him. "Are you okay little brother?"

Judas wheezed for breath.

"It's okay sweetie," JJ said next to him. "You're clean, no bites. Catch your breath. It'll be all right."

Judas took small breaths, struggling to breathe and grasping at his still rolling stomach. He noticed the package of peanut butter cups in his coat and a small smile crossed his lips. He pulled them out and handed them to JJ.

She laughed and smiled at him. "Oh my, Judas! Are those for me?"

"Mhm," he gasped in a breath and smiled back at her.

"That's so sweet, Judas. You know how to treat a woman." She threw a quick glance at Jonah, who grimaced and turned away. She turned back to Judas, looking him over. "Something's different about you."

"Is... that... good or bad?" he gasped.

Still smiling, JJ reached up and pulled the zipper on her coat halfway down, slowly revealing her cleavage and then her naked breasts. She pulled open the left side and slid the pack of candy into a pocket. "I'm gonna save these for later."

Behind them, Bobbie had gotten back up and now lumbered toward them, her own exposed breasts swaying back and forth.

"I'll deal with that," JJ said and pulled the Pink Lady from her thigh holster.

Judas grabbed her hand. "N-no!"

"What?" she looked at him with her eyes raised.

"It's Bobbie." He looked at Jonah, unable to take in enough oxygen to explain.

Jonah looked at the approaching dead woman. "No shit. Bobbie Burns?"

JJ, not knowing what was special about her, looked her over. The only thing special she could tell was that the woman's breasts were large and natural. They swayed back and forth in the open air. "What's so special about her?" JJ asked, tracking her with the barrel of her revolver.

Judas, still taking small gasping breaths, looked to Jonah.

"She was Judas's crush through middle school and high school."

"Too cute... to shoot," Judas wheezed.

"What?" JJ spun to glare at Judas, who still had his hand on her gun arm. She glanced over at Bobbie's breasts and JJ's cheeks burned. Her head snapped back to Judas. "Is it 'cause hers are real?"

Judas opened his mouth, but couldn't form a response. JJ

unzipped her coat the rest of the way. "You don't like these?" She shook her chest back and forth, making them jiggle. Then she removed his hand from her arm and stuck it right on her breast. "Feel it!" She mashed his hand around.

Judas's eyes went wide.

"Don't forget this one!" She moved his hand to the other breast.

Bobbie stepped closer.

JJ stood, sidestepped behind her, grabbed her by the hair and kicked the back of her knees. Bobbie collapsed right next to Judas, her head twisting back and forth as she grunted and growled, trying to get at JJ, who yanked her hair to keep her in place.

"Go ahead," JJ spat, "try 'em. Tell me—"

"Whoa, whoa," Jonah stood up from his brother's other side. "Cool off, sweet tits, we're here to kill zombies, not each other."

She glanced at Jonah, saw him smirking at her and scowled back at him. She slipped her revolver back into its holster. "You're right," she said through gritted teeth. She reached behind her and pulled Judas's knife from her belt. "Oh," she turned back to Judas. "I found this, by the way."

K-Thunk!

JJ slammed the knife into the side of Bobbie's head and watched as her body slumped over, the knife handle jutting up. "Thought you might like it back." JJ stood, then stormed outside past Nurse Janet who had come out of the bathroom at some point and stood with Nantucket, watching the scene.

Judas looked at Jonah. "I thought she'd make a cute girlfriend for Larry."

Jonah shook his head. "When it comes to women bro, any more than one is asking for problems."

"She's quite the pistol," Janet said, eyeing JJ as she stormed away.

Jonah, who was giving Judas a hand up, looked at Janet, nodding. "Oh yeah, she's like a pistol with a hair trigger and no safety."

Outside, JJ parked herself by a planter, puffing on a cigarette as she pulled out a peanut butter cup from the package Judas had given her.

Judas swayed as he stood and Jonah grabbed him by the shoulder. "What's the matter bro, did you get bit? Swallow some more chew?"

Judas shook his head. "Not bit, and I quit chewing."

"What?" Jonah tilted his head and stared at his brother.

"I quit. Though I could really use one right now."

"Why'd you do that?"

Judas put his hands on his knees, panting and looking out to where JJ leaned against the concrete planter.

Jonah thought about it and nodded. "I get it. So, why are you sick?"

Nantucket spoke up from behind them. "It was the Energy-Os, he ate a whole packet of them."

"He what?"

Judas stood up. "I ran out of mints. I've been using them to keep my mouth busy, so I ate that packet I got out of the vending machine. That stuff's like cocaine laced methamphetamine. I was so wired I could see the individual spectrums of light."

Jonah studied his brother and shook his head. "They give that stuff to kids?"

"Yeah, and more," Nurse Janet said. "Welcome to the new world order." She looked around at the chaos. "What happens now?"

"We put the rest of these poor souls out of their misery and then find out where this started. Our job's not done until we find the source and make sure it's contained," Jonah answered.

THEY FOUND Tommy's body in the carnage.

"This is who you said was sick first?"

"Yes," Janet answered, looking at the boy's green flesh and sighing. "He came into the office shortly after school started."

"Probably means this started at or near his home," Jonah said. "We'll need to get his address and go investigate."

"He lived outside of town on a farm, I think. I'll go pull his records and get an address for you." Janet walked away, then turned back. "Who cleans this up?"

"The principal will need to file a claim with the U.C.A."

"The principal's dead," Nurse Janet said. "You killed him earlier."

"Oh, that's right" Jonah said. "Well, we only do the exterminating. When the police get here, they'll call a clean-up service. Speaking of, I'd have thought your alarm system would've called them when the lockdown initiated?"

Janet shook her head. "There wasn't enough money in the budget for that module. Principal Hotchkins said someone in the office would have to call them if there was ever a need." She shrugged and wandered off toward the office.

Jonah turned to Judas. "I'm gonna go see if JJ's cooled off yet and if she wants to follow us to this farmhouse or..." he threw his hands up and made an 'I have no idea what to expect' face.

"Thanks, bro," Judas said and looked over to where he spied Nantucket talking to a boy at the end of the hall. He walked in their direction.

"What happened out here?" the boy asked her.

"We made a bomb to kill the zombies," Nantucket answered.

"You made that bomb?" the boy asked.

"Yeah, me and Mr. Judas. He's one of the Zombie Exterminators."

"That's so cool!" The boy turned to Judas as he walked up. "Hi, my name's Nick. That's so awesome that you made that bomb. Thanks for saving us."

Judas raised his eyebrows and looked over at Nantucket. "Nick?"

"Yeah, that's me. I was in the bathroom with your brother." Nick stuck out his hand.

Nat's nostrils flared.

"Mr. Judas, would it be possible to get your autograph?" the boy asked.

Judas studied the boy a moment, then reached out and took his hand, holding it tight in his own. "Listen Nick. I think there's something you should know." He squeezed tighter.

Nick pulled back but found he couldn't move. Judas gripped his arm tight.

"I didn't make that bomb. She did." He nodded at Nantucket. "She's the one that saved your ass. *All* of our asses. Do you know why she knew how to make a bomb?"

"No..." Nick looked at Nantucket who bit her lip.

"I don't either," Judas said. "But while we were making it she told me the story of a kid who was bullying her. A really mean boy. Now, one could say she might have gotten upset and put her smarts into figuring out how to get back at that kid. She might've been planning something not very nice herself." He shrugged. "Maybe not. But, it sure would be for the best if she wasn't being picked on around here and had more time to focus her attentions on getting an education and maybe not so much on how to make bombs, wouldn't you say?"

Nick, whose eyes were already as wide as could be, stared straight at Judas. "Uh-huh."

"Good. That's what I was thinking too. So I'll tell you what." He let get of the boy's hand, reached behind him and pulled out his wallet. He removed two of the brothers' business cards, flipped them over and then looked up.

Nantucket held a pen out in the air before her.

Judas smiled. "Thank you! That's exactly what I needed."

"So," Judas turned back to Nick. "Let's make a deal. I'll give you my autograph and you'll keep an eye on Ms. Nantucket, the Zombie Slaying Savior of Savini Charter School and make sure no-one's picking on her." Judas scribbled on the card's back and handed it to Nick. He did the same on the other and gave it and the pen back to Nantucket. "You both have my number now, so if there's any problems and you need help, you can call me. How's that sound?"

"Uhhh..." Nick muttered.

Nat beamed.

"S-sure, thing. Mr. Judas." He stared at the card and inched back. "Um, can I go now?"

"It was nice meeting you, Nick," Judas said and nodded.

Nick turned and took off down the hall.

Tears ran down Nantucket's face as she smiled up at Judas. He dropped to one knee in front of her. "Hey," he said smiling back.

She laughed, put her arms around his neck and hugged him. "Thank you for being my hero, Mr. Judas."

❧

OUTSIDE, JJ had been found by the group of children Jonah had helped out of the bathroom window. They sat in a circle, with Xanadu in the middle, wagging his tail and turning to each of them as they giggled his name and reached out to pet him.

"You were right Mr. Jonah," the little dark haired girl, Emily said. "This dog is awesome."

He smiled. "Xanadu is something else, that's for sure, and so's his mistress." He turned his attention to JJ. "How are you doing?"

She looked up at him; hair covered her right eye, but her left eye was wide and her face wore a tight grimace. "I'm fine."

Jonah picked up JJ's pack of cigarettes off the planter and took one out. He lit it, took a deep drag and smiled.

"Mr. Jonah," one kid said, "You can't do that here."

"Yeah," JJ said, lifting a half smoked, extinguished cigarette from the grass beside her.

"Kids," Jonah looked over his shoulder at the giant hole in the side of the school, "sometimes adults break the rules." He reached out his hand to JJ. "C'mon honey. Let's walk a moment."

She took his hand, but as he helped her up, she said, "Don't honey me," and as they turned away from the kids, she growled, "and no sweet tits either."

They walked a few yards away, and JJ pulled out a fresh cigarette which Jonah lit for her.

"What's the matter?" he asked.

She scrunched up her face, bit her lip and shook her head. "I got jealous. That..." She made a series of funny faces. "He was just gonna let that big-breasted bimbo on his lap and let her eat him."

"She was his childhood crush, JJ."

"And now she's a dead zombie."

"I know, I know. Judas wasn't quite himself. He was on some sort of stimulant they give the kids, and he quit using chewing tobacco."

"He what? Why?"

Jonah looked her in the eyes and raised his eyebrows. "He wants to be a better man. He wants you to like him."

She looked at the cigarette in her own hand and flicked it to the ground. "Dammit. I don't want him to change. I like him," she stopped and took Jonah's three-fingered hand in hers, "I like you both... just the way you are."

He smiled at her. "We're gonna head out to a farmhouse where we think this started. Want to come along?"

She smiled back and took a deep breath. "Yeah, I do. Oh, and by the way, I've got a package for you in my car."

"A package?"

"Yeah, me and Judas got you a little something."

Jonah squinted at her as his brow furrowed. "You've got me curious."

"Ah, sugar, if you haven't realized by now, I'm full of surprises."

PART XVI - OF BOYS, MEN & DOGS

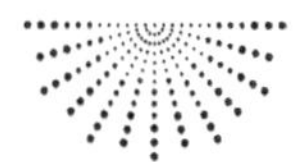

JJ POPPED OPEN the trunk of her Charger and reached behind the leather satchel, grabbing the small wrapped package.

Jonah, who was peering over her shoulder, caught sight of the riding crop and panties sticking out of the bag and said, "Interesting overnight accessories you have there."

She grinned up at him as she closed the trunk and handed him the package, not saying a word.

He looked at the box, turned it around and weighed it in his hand. "What is it?"

"Something Judas and I got you. Where is he, anyway?"

"He's back talking to a couple of the kids still."

"Well, go ahead and open it, he already knows what it is."

Jonah pulled the wrapping paper away, revealing a small white box with a picture of a phone on it.

"It's a smartphone!" JJ beamed.

Jonah opened his mouth, preparing to protest but thought better of it. "I'm not sure I'm gonna have a clue what to do with this."

"Oh, don't worry, they're easy to figure out. If you're having

Judas drive, you'll have it mastered by the time we get there. How's he doing by the way?"

Jonah continued staring at the box, uncertain what to do with it. "Better. There's a lot less for him to concentrate on without Sasha's stick shift. I'm going to have him take his driver's test again before we have to return the rental."

"How many times has he taken it?"

"Five."

"Oh!" Her eyes widened.

"Yeah."

"How does someone fail it that many times?"

"Well, the first time wasn't so much his fault. It was a hot summer day and they drove with the windows open. Judas was just supposed to pull into a spot and park, it wasn't even parallel parking. A bee flew in and he was wearing shorts, the bee went up his leg. He freaked, slammed on the gas as he swatted at it. Sasha charged ahead, hit forty plus miles an hour, went off a small embankment and ended up in a fountain at the city park. Judas jumped out of the truck, pulled his shorts down and was scream-ing, 'Do you see it? Do you see it?' Kids were playing near the fountain. Nobody got hurt, but the proctor hadn't seen the bee, he thought Judas was nuts and a terrible driver."

"On no," JJ held her hands to her mouth.

"Yeah. When he went for his retest, it was the same proctor. He wouldn't even get in the truck with Judas. After that, Judas was a complete mess every time he went back. The next time, with a new proctor, he was so nervous, doing everything he could to drive safe, he pulled up behind what he believed was a line of traffic and stopped. They sat queued there for five minutes before the proctor pointed out to him that it was one thing to be a polite driver but another thing entirely to get in line behind parked cars and not realize they were empty."

JJ guffawed, bursting out from behind her hands. "Oh no, I shouldn't be laughing. Poor Judas."

HEAVY METAL MUSIC thumped as the red Prius drove along the road leading out of town. Judas bounced his head to the beat, a big grin on his face. "I sure enjoy being able to pick the music."

Jonah puffed on his pipe and stared blankly at the screen on his new phone. "Huh?" he turned at the sound of his brother's voice.

Judas reached over and lowered the volume. "I said, I enjoy being able to pick the music."

Jonah nodded and smiled at his brother. "Driving comes with its rewards." His gaze returned to the icon-filled screen before him.

Judas looked in the rearview mirror, saw JJ following in her Charger and asked, "What'd she say, Jonah? Is she mad at me?"

Jonah blew a long stream of smoke out the window, then tapped his pipe against the side of the car, emptying the charred bowl. "She's upset, but not with you. She's upset with herself because she felt insecure. She likes you and was jealous of your old feelings toward Bobbie."

"She likes me?" he beamed and sat up straighter, smiling into the mirror and hoping she could see it.

Jonah nodded. "Yep, she does."

They drove in silence a moment, then Jonah clicked the phone off and spoke again. "Look Judas, I've been thinking... seeing Bobbie, I remember how upset you were when I took her out on that date in high school. I shouldn't have done that and I'm sorry."

Judas swallowed and cleared his throat. "Thank you Jonah, and I uh..." he reached up and rubbed the couple days' worth of growth on his chin. "I'm sorry about rolling that stink bomb under the—"

"No you're not," Jonah barked and, after a pause, he spoke softer, "and you shouldn't be."

Judas glanced over and nodded, clicking the wipers on as rain fell in a pitter-patter against the window.

"So look, like I was saying," Jonah continued, "I've been thinking and I'm uh, I'm gonna get outta the way."

Judas's head snapped in his brother's direction, eyebrows raised. "What do you mean?"

"I'm not gonna pursue JJ, I'm gonna stay away from her and let you two..." he shrugged and reloaded his pipe with tobacco.

Judas shook his head, eyes scrunched, staring ahead. "You what? How do you think she's gonna feel about that? She likes you too, you know?"

"Yeah, I know but," Jonah shook his own head, "We don't understand women very well, so I'll just be distant and such and mention another woman or something when she's around. Let her know I'm not interested."

Judas's eyes shot wide open and he accidentally tapped the brakes, causing the Prius to lurch. "No, Jonah, don't do that! You saw how she reacted to Bobbie."

Jonah let out a laugh. "Yeah, I don't know then. I'll just keep my distance and let you two be."

Judas nodded. "Thank you, Jonah. I'm not sure what to say. She's a helluva woman."

Jonah shrugged again. "Me either. Except we shouldn't ever mention anything regarding Dr. N. to her either. I don't believe she'd be thrilled to learn of our relationship with her."

Judas laughed. "Oh no! Definitely, not." He reached down and cranked up the music.

IN THE CHARGER BEHIND THEM, JJ stroked Xanadu's head, twisting the hair on his neck between her fingers with one hand and flicking her cigarette out the window with the other. She steered with her knee.

"I don't know what to think of those two! They drive me mad.

One moment I think they're brave, sweet and adorable, but the next they're a couple of dim-witted oafs!"

She had twisted his hair tight around her fingers, tugging the skin. Xanadu looked up and let out a bark. "Ruff."

"Sorry boy," she said, letting go of his hair and patting his head. "What do you think, are they good guys?"

"Ruff!"

"Hmm." She lit another cigarette and drove. "What about Jonah? He's rough, bossy and can be a bit arrogant, but he's big and handsome."

"Ruff!"

"Ok, and Judas? He's cute, funny and has a big heart. It's like they're opposite sides of the same coin."

"Ruff!"

"Ruff?" JJ said. "That's all you've got?" She shook her head. "I'm trying to decide if one or both of them will break my heart, and all you've got is *ruff*? Whose side are you on?"

Xanadu slunk lower in the passenger seat and whimpered.

They were driving through a wooded area with the pavement ending and the road becoming a puddle and pothole-filled obstacle course. Getting close to the farm. "I just need some kinda sign. One? Both? Neither?"

The brothers' Prius drove around a bend, disappearing from her sight for a moment. She stepped on the gas to catch up with them but had to slam on her brakes suddenly as a pair of stags, with large sets of antlers, bounded from the woods and across the road before her.

The car screeched to a halt in a cloud of dust, and Xanadu found himself flung to the floor. He let out a soft yelp.

"Oh no!" JJ unbuckled herself and dove across the center console to scoop him up. "Are you okay, boy? Anything broken? I'm so sorry! I'm so distracted by myself..." She looked up at the road; the pair of deer were gone and the road before her was empty.

"Dammit." A lone tear ran down her cheek, but she smiled as Xanadu snuggled into her lap and licked it from her face. "Is that your way of telling me you're the only one for me?"

He didn't answer, only curled up in her lap and closed his eyes.

She took a deep breath, looked at the dirt road ahead and said, "Better get moving. I don't know which of them I need, but I know they both need me."

She punched it and tore off after them, racing to catch up. By the time she did, they were parked before the farmhouse, standing in front of the Prius, with half a dozen men facing them, shotguns and rifles aimed at their lovable, infuriating faces.

PART XVII - FARMHOUSE FRESH

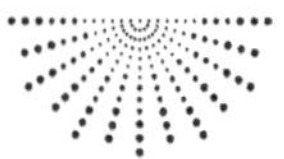

As the brothers pulled up to the farmhouse, they were glad to find a group of six living men. That was, until those men turned around and leveled their guns toward the car.

Jonah muttered under his breath. "Stay here, keep your gun handy."

"It's in the back, Jonah!"

Jonah already had his door open. He shook his head; at least he had Brutus.

A short, heavyset man in a black and red, checkered flannel shirt and suspenders stepped forward. He looked sixtyish and like he'd been farming his entire life. "Tell your lover there to get out too, hands up."

"Look—" Jonah started.

The man turned the barrel of his shotgun at Jonah. "Now."

Jonah put his hands up, turned to Judas and nodded for him to get out.

Judas got out, put his hands in the air and walked to stand by his brother.

"Now," the older man said, "who the fuck are you?"

"I'm Jonah, this is my brother Judas. We're Zom—"

"I don't care who you hybrid driving homos are, I want to know why you're here!"

"Well then, why'd you ask—," Judas started.

Jonah used the elbow of his raised arm to smack Judas on the side of the head. "Sir, we're Zombie Exterminators and we're here because—"

"Bullshit. Everyone knows they aren't real. It's just another part of our incorporated government's way of keeping the people scared. Keep them buying and keep them from asking questions."

"Look, sir, I'm no fan of the U.C.A. either, but they are real and that's why we're here. There was an outbreak at the Savini Charter School this morning. One of the Tucker kids was sick and—"

"Jonah," Judas motioned toward the back of a pick-up, where a man lay clutching his arm. He was pale, sweating and, obvious to the brothers, very near turning.

Jonah turned back to the heavyset man. "May I ask why all of you are here pointing guns at the Tuckers' home?"

The man spat. "These rotten pig fuckers. They killed all of our cows, and when Chuck came over to confront them, one of 'em bit him."

Jonah nodded, finally getting a better grasp on the situation. "What did they do to your cows?"

"I don't know," the man growled. "We woke up this morning to find the whole lot dead in the pasture. They were green and bloated and there was this residue covering the ground. It was green too. We followed it, it led right to Dale Tucker's piece of shit Fiat 411R diesel tractor. It looked as if he'd dug up an old septic tank, punctured it and tried to roll it downhill onto our property. Only, his Italian piece of shit broke and it spilled everywhere. There's a big puddle of it sitting out there in the field."

"Sir," Jonah began, trying to be respectful and bring calm to the situation, "I don't think that was a septic tank. We're here because Tommy Tucker was sick at school. He died and came back as a zombie. He was green, just like you described, and I think maybe the whole family got exposed to some experimental chemical, it turned them into—"

"Yeah, yeah. I get what you're trying to pull, and if that was the case, why ain't my cows coming back to life and starting the cowpocalypse or something?"

"I can't say, sir. I don't understand how it works as I've only seen it once before and it wasn't being used on animals."

The man in the truck bed convulsed, foam forming around his lips. The old heavyset man rushed over. "Chuck!" he shouted. "C'mon brother, you okay?"

Chuck's body continued to jerk about a moment before going still. A bubbling green foam ran from his mouth and down his chin.

"God dammit! You pig fucking Tuckers!" the man shouted at the farm house. "I'm gonna kill you all!"

"Jonah," Judas whispered, "What are we gonna do?"

"I don't know. We can't let them go in there."

"Maybe we should let 'em," Judas shrugged. "They've got enough guns."

"Maybe so. But do they have enough brains? They'll likely get themselves killed."

"That's gonna happen as soon as the brother turns. Can't warn 'em. They never listen. People always got to find out for themselves." Judas shook his head.

Just then, a car door was deliberately slammed behind them. All eyes turned to see JJ setting Xanadu on the ground next to her Charger. She had the orange t-shirt with its v-neck back on, and her jacket hung open, exposing her cleavage for all to view. She paused long enough to make sure everyone got an eye full before standing up. The men pointing their guns at Jonah and Judas shifted their attention though not their barrels.

"Did I hear you boys say you were cow farmers?"

"Yes we are," said one man with a rifle, stepping forward and standing taller.

JJ smiled at him. "My Xanadu just loves moo-moos! Don't you Xanadu?" She bent over to scratch the top of his head and give the farmers another view of her acreage. "Wanna see the moo-moos?"

Xanadu perked up, looking at her and glancing around with anticipation.

"He loves to chase them. He'll charge after 'em and then they'll charge after him. When I'm driving and see them in a pasture, I'll shout, 'look at the moo-moos' and he'll get super excited, jump up and put his paws on the window and stare at them." Both her and Xanadu came closer.

"All of our cows are dead, miss," the heavyset man said, standing next to the bed of the truck. "The Tuckers," he pointed his thumb over his shoulder at the house behind him, "killed 'em."

"Oh no, that's terrible," JJ said with every bit of southern sugary sweetness she could muster. "Why'd they do a thing like that?"

The man let out a bitter laugh and spat on the ground. "They're jealous, of course. They sit over here with their filthy pigs, doing filthy things, and knowing how everyone talks about 'em… they see us living all clean, having the high life, and they just couldn't take it no more, so they went an' poisoned 'em."

"Oh," JJ put her hand over her mouth. "That's awful!" She reached down and slid her hand behind her back. "What's your name, sir?"

"My name's Robert Carlisle. My brother and I own Carlisle's Cows—" He stopped, remembering his brother, just as the body in the truck stirred and moaned. "Chuck?" Robert's eyes widened. "Thank the Holy Spirit!"

Chuck, his eyes empty white clouds, sat up and a mouthful of greenish-red goo spilled out to rush down his chin.

"I thought you were gone," Robert said and reached for his brother.

"Mr. Carl—," Jonah started.

Chuck's eyes turned toward his brother and his mouth opened with a hiss. He shot forward, grabbing his brother by the arm, teeth gnashing, and he pulled it toward his hungering mouth.

Blam!

The pink lady boomed, blowing Chuck's head to pieces and showering his brother in a red mist. JJ looked at Jonah and Judas, raising her eyebrows in panic. "Oops," she mouthed.

Judas mouthed back, "Nice shot!"

Xanadu, seemingly unaffected by the noise, sat in the dirt to watch. He looked as all did, first at Robert, sputtering and stammering as the body of his now twice dead brother slumped over in the bed of the truck. Then, to the shattered rear window where the tinkling shards of glass from the blasted out window fell in pieces.

Robert spun to glare at JJ, his shotgun raising. "You killed my brother!"

"Now look here," Jonah stepped forward, putting himself between the barrel and JJ. "Your brother was going to take a bite out of you and what just happened to him, woulda happened to you next. She saved your life."

"She shot him!"

"Yeah, she did. She's a great shot too. Got him right in the head, which is how you kill zombies."

"He was my brother!"

"I know sir," Jonah softened his tone. "We just came from a school where adults and children were infected, and we're here to help."

The man turned and looked at the remains of his brother, a heaving sob tearing through him.

Jonah stepped forward. "I'm sorry for your loss, sir. I know how hard it is to understand. We've seen this kind of thing before. Sometimes, there isn't time to wait and explain. You have to take the shot and hope for the best. You should get that blood cleaned off before it's too late; let us take care of the Tuckers, we're professionals."

The man stood there sobbing a moment, then turned to scowl at Jonah before barking at a young blond boy, barely out of his teens. "Shawn!"

"Yes, Pop?"

"You stay out here. Keep your gun trained on that one." He pointed a pudgy finger at JJ. "And if either of these two homos make a move toward you or the house, you shoot! Understand me?"

"Yes sir!" the blond boy said and stepped around to get a clear line of sight on her.

JJ slipped her gun back into its holster.

Judas leaned into Jonah and whispered, "Jonah?"

Jonah shook his head and shrugged.

Xanadu bared his teeth, got up walked over to sit in front of JJ, staring at the young man with the gun and growling.

Robert wiped the blood, tears, and rain from his face, spat at Jonah's feet and spoke to his men. "We're gonna deal with this ourselves boys. Make sure you're locked and loaded, then follow me."

Jonah, Judas, and JJ stood in the rain and watched as the men lined up at the front door. Robert was sniffling, causing Jonah to wonder if he was still crying or if the toxins from his brother's blood had spread the infection already.

Robert aimed his shotgun at the front door and fired both barrels into it, leaving a pair of large holes, but the door remained closed. He reloaded, then reached down, turning the door knob. The door opened. He motioned for the others to head in.

The group of men charged past, and Robert followed after a pause to grope at this stomach.

Shots rang out.

"I got one! I got one!" A voice shouted, followed moments later by screams as evidently, something got him.

The blond boy turned to stare at the front door, eyes widening as both the number of gunshots and screams increased.

"Jonah, are we just gonna stand here?" Judas asked.

"We don't have much choice at the moment." Jonah looked over at their guard and raised his voice. "Unless you're willing to let us go help?"

The blonde's attention snapped back to the trio, his face trembling. "You stay right where you are. You heard my Pops!"

"Yeah," Judas said, "pretty sure that was him screaming a moment ago."

The shotgun swung from JJ to Judas but his attention turned back to the house as more screams than gunshots were ringing out.

Xanadu stood up and trotted from JJ's feet toward the young man.

"That's a mighty big house the Tuckers have. How big of a family were they?" Jonah asked.

The boy glanced at him, then back at the house. "There was twelve of them that lived there, plus a few wee ones. Couple of farm hands now and again too." He looked down as Xanadu approached.

"Hey! What's your dog doing?" he shouted at JJ. "Does he bite?" His shotgun swung to point at Xanadu.

"No!" JJ shouted and broke out in a run. "I'll get him! Don't shoot!"

The boy glanced up as JJ ran toward him. With her jacket open, her breasts bounced wildly and he didn't notice Xanadu lifting his leg until he heard the stream of urine pouring off his boots. He glared down just as JJ arrived to squat at his feet.

"Xanadu, that's no way to make friends!" she scolded and looked up into the boy's eyes, but noticed his were looking lower. Boys, so easy to distract. "I'm so sorry, mister." She smiled at him. "He's usually a good boy, he just doesn't like it when people point guns at his momma." She shrugged, pushing her breasts up and together.

Shawn stared at them, his mouth opening and closing like a

suckling newborn, trying to form words. A shadow fell across his face as Judas walked up and clocked him with an angry fist. The boy fell onto his back in the mud, out cold.

"What the dog's saying is, never point a gun at our girl."

JJ stood up with a wide grin. "Thank you. We sure make a great team!"

"You're welcome," Judas smiled back and laughed. "If there was time, I'd join Xanadu."

JJ turned and caught her pup relieving himself again. This time straight onto the blonde's face.

"Xanadu, stop it!" she said, biting back a mischievous smile.

Jonah pulled a small length of rope from his pocket. He rolled the boy over, bound his hands and spoke to Judas. "Help me put him inside this truck. Don't want any roamers to get him while he can't defend himself."

"Good thinking, Jonah."

They tossed the boy onto the bucket seat of an old Ford and closed the door.

"Let's load up. Judas, pop the trunk, we're going in with every-thing we can carry this time."

PART XVIII - THE FARMING DEAD

JJ SET Xanadu on the passenger seat of the Charger and patted his head. "You're a good boy. Thank you for standing up for me." She closed the door and zipped her coat up. Reaching into her pocket, she pulled out a bullet and replaced the one she'd fired.

The brothers were strapping on their body armor at the trunk of the Prius. Jonah puffed on his cigar and Judas popped another mint in his mouth.

"What's that all about?" JJ asked as she walked over.

Judas looked up from tightening a strap, the mint held between his teeth. "Hmm?"

"The mint?"

"Oh," he pulled it into his mouth and pushed it against his cheek. "I quit chew."

"You did?"

"Mhm," he smiled at her, his teeth clean.

Jonah stepped away, walking to the front of the car.

"How come?"

Judas's cheeks turned pink, and he squirmed where he stood. He took another mint out of his pocket and stuck it in his mouth.

He spoke, but his words were unintelligible through the two hard candies.

"What are you doing?" JJ asked.

Judas sputtered then spit one of them out. "I'm trying to keep myself from saying anything stupid."

"By stuffing your mouth with mints?"

"Mhm."

"Why'd you quit chewing Judas?"

"I, um, well. I don't want you to see me as some kind of ick mouth. Women don't like men that chew tobacco."

JJ watched him a moment. "First, I'd never call you or anyone an ick mouth. Except maybe a zombie. My first kiss called me that when I was thirteen because I had bad teeth as a kid. I punched him in the face and knocked out one of his. And second," she stepped closer. "I don't need you to change who you are, Judas. No, it's not healthy and I don't cherish the thought of what it might do to your sweet face, but I love with all the love my little heart has. And I love you for being you, both of you." She stepped in close to Judas, looking up into his eyes and smiling.

Judas's mouth opened, jaw trembling. He could smell her sweet perfume and ached to feel the warmth of her lips on his.

Jonah, who'd been watching, turned away and focused his attention on the front of the farmhouse.

JJ grabbed the sides of Judas's armored vest and lifted herself up on her tiptoes, planting a kiss. "Don't forget it."

Heat spread across his cheeks and he glanced over at Jonah's back. "Thank you," he said. "You're an amazing woman."

She smiled back at him and reached across to squeeze his hand. "Now, I'm gonna go give Jonah a kiss too, so you both know how I feel."

A lump sank from his throat to his stomach, stealing his voice in a mutter.

"What's that sweetie?"

"Um," Judas fidgeted, sweat forming around the brim of his hat and his forehead. "He said, he uh, was gonna let me have you."

Her face flipped from a sweet smile with soft eyes, to burning embers and a snarl. "He what?" she shouted.

Jonah's head snapped around to find JJ stepping away from Judas and turning toward him. *Oh, shit.*

She stomped her way across the mud in his direction. "So, you're gonna decide who I like and who I don't, huh?"

His hands flew up and he took a step back. "Now calm down just a minute, JJ."

"No!" Her right pointer finger flew up in his face. "Don't ever tell a woman to calm down. And don't tell me, or him, who I get to choose to be with. He—" she pointed at Judas, "doesn't have to change a damn thing for me to like him. And you—" she stabbed her finger into his chest armor, "I might just decide not to like all on my own."

She strode passed him, heading toward the front door of the farmhouse.

In the Charger, Xanadu hopped up on the seat, placing his paws on the window ledge, and whined.

Jonah turned and glared at Judas, who threw his hands up and shrugged. "I don't know how to talk to her. She either smiles and kisses me or turns around and wants to shoot someone."

Jonah couldn't help but laugh. "Ain't that the truth. C'mon, let's get after her before she clears the whole place herself."

The brothers ran to catch up with JJ, who stopped a few feet from the open door. Groans and the sound of feeding came from inside. They stopped behind her as a large shadow fell across the doorway and the bloody bulk of Robert Carlisle stumbled out and fell to the ground before them. He oozed blood from the various bite marks and torn flesh that covered his body.

"Help me," he called out. "They came from everywhere. They got my son, they got..." he heaved out a giant sob. "They got us all."

Another form appeared at the doorway. This one was a tall thin man they hadn't seen before. His skin carried the green pallor of the poisonous infection that had turned him and his family into flesh hungry monsters.

"Judas, lure him off to the side. We'll make them come to us, hopefully, one at a time, and we can take them out, here in the open."

"You got it, bro! I dig your thinking. No tight quarters or surprises to worry about and less mess to clean up."

Jonah bent before Mr. Carlisle. "Sir—"

The old man stopped sobbing and looked up. "I know. You don't have to say it. I get it now. I saw them in there, what they looked like, what they did to one another. I shoulda listened."

"C'mon you rotter," Judas taunted behind them, getting the attention of the dead farmer and drawing him away from the entry.

"There's no cure?" the man asked.

"No," Jonah said, "I'm sorry. Once bitten, there's little to nothing that can be done."

"My other son, Shaun? Where is he? You didn't hurt him, did you?"

"No. He's safe. Just tied up in the truck."

"Thank you. Thank you. He's all that's left. Please make sure he doesn't t—"

Blam!

Judas's gun blasted and the thin farmer's body dropped to the ground.

Mr. Carlisle struggled to his feet and finished his sentence. "Make sure he doesn't see me like this. I don't want to be one of them." He turned and lumbered off to where Judas stood with the dead zombie. He slumped to his knees before Judas. "Make me next please, before it happens."

Judas looked over at Jonah, shaking his head. "I..."

Two more shapes appeared in the doorway.

Jonah grabbed JJ's hand. "Back away, let's lead them over by Mr. Carlisle."

JJ pulled her hand back. "I can walk away by myself."

"JJ, don't be like—"

"Like what? Rejected? You said you didn't want me!"

The two shapes emerged from the house; an elderly couple dressed in blood-splattered nightgowns, probably the patriarch and matriarch of the Tucker family. They turned instantly toward the arguing voices of JJ and Jonah.

"I didn't say I didn't want you." Jonah glanced over his shoulder at Judas, who stood staring down at Mr. Carlisle at his feet. Mr. Carlisle had his eyes closed and his hands raised before him in a steeple.

"Yes, you did." She turned her head away, her hair snapping over her face.

"JJ look," he stopped, grabbing her by the arm and pulling her to face him.

She tugged her arm, but his grip was firm and he held her fast.

"Judas is crazy about you. I can see it in him, and I don't want him to get hurt. I said I wouldn't pursue you, that I'd let him—"

"What about you, Jonah? How do you feel?" She looked into his eyes, searching. "And what about *me*, Jonah? What about how I feel?"

Jonah's mouth opened, words not forming the way he'd have liked them to. Finally, he sputtered. "I like you, it's just Juda—"

"Guys," Judas shouted. They glanced up and saw him pointing past them. The elderly couple was almost on them and another one, a young dead child, still in its pajamas, was coming out the door next.

JJ used the moment to slip out of Jonah's grip and turned to face the body of the old farmer as it approached. "How about you?" she taunted. "Do you like me?"

The zombie growled as it approached, mouth gnashing at the air.

"I thought so," she said and stepped away in the opposite direction.

Jonah did the same, leading the elderly female a safe distance away. They put them to rest with quick shots and Jonah walked over to Judas. He pointed to the young pajama-wearing zombie that had followed the elderly couple out. "Go take care of that one Judas, I'll help Mr. Carlisle here."

Judas looked at the boy and then at Mr. Carlisle, whose labored breathing signaled the end was soon, and he didn't know which option was worse. "Ok, bro," he said shaking his head. "Sometimes this job isn't a lot of fun."

"No, it's not." Jonah shook his head, lifted Brutus to Mr. Carlisle's temple and pulled the trigger.

From there, the trio took turns leading the dead from the house. They came in a steady stream for a few minutes, but never more than could be handled. Mr. Carlisle's family and ranch hands were the last to emerge, having taken a while to turn.

Aside from the taunts to lead the dead in a given direction, they said nothing to one another.

Finally, when a few minutes had passed and no more of the farming dead emerged, JJ asked. "What now?"

"We need to go sweep the house. Make sure that's the last of them and then go investigate the source. Everyone reload," Jonah said.

PART XIX - POTS & PANS

INSIDE, the farmhouse looked more like a slaughterhouse. Blood and carnage reigned. Half eaten appendages lay on the floor next to pools of green and red blood. A few partially devoured corpses that couldn't move their bodies, swung their arms around, trying to grab at the fresh meat they saw in Jonah, Judas, and JJ.

The group made quick work of the dead they found remaining until they came to a closed door off the kitchen. Inside they could hear multiple forms banging about.

"How many you think are in there, Jonah?" Judas asked.

"I can't tell. Sounds like a couple at least."

"How do you want to handle this?"

Jonah looked around the large white kitchen. There was a small table with two chairs and little else. "You two grab those chairs, be ready to use them to hold them back if there's more than I can handle."

A loud frustrated sounding groan came from behind the door. Jonah wrapped his left hand around the doorknob and held Brutus high. He waited as Judas and JJ picked up the wooden chairs and lifted them so that the legs pointed out before them.

"I feel like a lion tamer," Judas joked.

JJ laughed, which made Judas smile.

Jonah felt a knot in his stomach and bit on his lip, turning away before either of them could see his discomfort. He took a deep breath, turned back and mouthed, "Ready?"

They both nodded, looking more relaxed than they had for the last hour.

Jonah let out the breath, twisted the knob and opened the door.

Behind it, he discovered an overloaded pantry, heavy with the scent of aged goods stored too long. A single light bulb, mounted in the ceiling, lit the small room and cast shadows. The shelves teetered with large cans of food, boxes, and ancient dust covered canning jars that looked as if they'd been there since before the Great Depression.

On the ground was a single zombie, its focus intent on a box on the floor in a back corner, under the bottom shelf. It growled and strained, its arm reaching to get at whatever was inside the box. The box sat behind a few large, heavy bags of flour and sugar.

"Hey, meat sack," Jonah called out.

The zombie snapped its head around. It had been a middle aged man, a large chunk of its neck was missing. Seeing something more easily accessible than whatever it had been trying to get at, it turned and stood.

"How many are there, Jonah?" Judas asked.

"Just one," Jonah said, stepping back from the opening. There was another door off the kitchen which led outside. Jonah opened it and turned back to the pantry. "C'mon now, follow me." He waved his arms around and kept the zombie from noticing his brother and JJ.

The zombie followed Jonah.

JJ looked at Judas who, like her, still held her chair at the ready. A loud clang of metal on metal from the pantry made them both jump. They stared at each other with wide eyes. *Surely, Jonah hadn't missed one?*

Judas stepped in front of the door and peered in. The floor was clear, there was nothing to see, then the clank of metal on metal sounded again.

"What is it?" JJ whispered from behind him.

"I don't know. There's something back in the corner." He fumbled around in his pocket and pulled out a flashlight, clicking it on.

"Another zombie?"

"No," Judas glanced back at her as they heard the distant blast of Brutus. "This is something else. Maybe someone hiding."

He moved in closer, ready to find out what it was, but jumped when JJ touched his arm.

"Sorry," she said, moving in closer. "I didn't want you to be alone. What if this is where it started?" Her voice shook at the last bit.

Judas shook his head. "No, we learned from Mr. Carlisle when we first got here that it started out in the pasture. This," he gulped, "is something different."

JJ's fingers tightened around his sleeve as they inched closer.

Judas hadn't been scared before, but something about JJ's presence, the way she clung to his arm for protection and then the clang of metal on metal, set the little hairs on the back of his neck tingling. Something definitely moved below. He cast the light into the corner, reached down and tugged one of the heavy flour sacks out of the way.

A large and old cardboard box sat on the tiled pantry floor, crammed under the shelf. He pulled it out. The back corner was crushed and a large hole opened where it caused the flaps to separate. A lone eye stared out at them.

Judas rested on his knees and turned to look at JJ as she knelt beside him. They heard the sound of Jonah's boots entering the kitchen.

"Open it," JJ whispered.

Judas put the flashlight in his mouth and reached out with his free hands to pull the flaps of the box open.

"Ooh!" JJ let out a soft gasp as the cardboard peeled back.

"Mew?"

Inside the box, two over-weight kittens, one gray and black scrunched low at the bottom of a large pot, the other, gray and white sat in a shallow pan.

JJ burst into giggles. "Oh my gosh. They're so big, I bet they say moo instead of meow" She reached in, scooped them up and held them against her chest. They purred and licked at her cheeks. She beamed at Judas. "My hero!" she said and kissed his cheek, which instantly turned red and warm.

He pulled the flashlight from his mouth and said, "Jonah saved them. I only opened the box."

She stood, cradling the cats in her arms, and turned to see Jonah standing in the doorway watching. His face was expression-less. She walked up to him and held up the kittens. "Jonah, meet Pots and Pans. Sometimes we don't choose our families. They choose us." She raised up on her toes and kissed his unmoving lips. "I choose the two of you." She glanced back at Judas. "We're just gonna have to figure it out." She stepped past Jonah and strode outside with the kittens.

PART XX - TOXIC RELATIONSHIPS

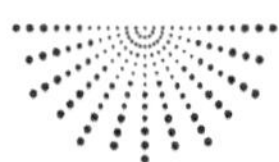

"THIS IS WHAT CAUSED THE OUTBREAK?" JJ asked, reaching back and tightening the strap on her gas mask.

Jonah nodded. "Yeah, from what Mr. Carlisle said, one of the Tuckers' accidentally uncovered this tank on his property, ruptured it and..." he motioned to the dead cows.

"But where'd it come from?" she asked.

Jonah looked at Judas, who stood a little ways away with Xanadu. "Corporations have been known to illegally dump their problems before. Remember Erin Brockovich?"

"What kind of company would put a toxic, zombie creating poison out here?"

Jonah stepped down the hill, moving closer. The tank, with its rust spots and worn paint, appeared to have been underground for several years. The dirt caked on it had been partially washed away by the rain. On the far side, he found what he was looking for. A symbol he suspected would be there but had rather hoped wasn't.

Two letter N's, intertwined and wrapped in a circle. He nodded at Judas and pointed at it. Judas's gas mask bobbed in acknowledgment, then side to side in disgust.

"What is it?" JJ asked, looking between them. "What's going on?"

Jonah walked up from the remains of the storage tank and lifted his mask. "It's owned by the company we used to work for."

"What do you mean?"

"It's how we got our start as zombie exterminators. We used to work for this scientist, sh—"

"Dr. Nitsau," Judas blurted out. "The Nitsau Corporation. They performed experiments on different zombie causing agents. We did security, body guarding and clean-up."

JJ's face scrunched up. "The Nitsau Corporation? Wasn't that the one whose CEO went missing a few years back?"

"Yeah," Judas shot a wide-eyed glance at Jonah. "That's the one."

"What was a pharmaceutical company doing researching zombies?"

Jonah & Judas both turned to look at the tank, neither willing to answer the question.

Dear Reader,

Thank you for taking the time to read this work of fiction. As a writer, one of the greatest rewards of writing, is to hear from my readers and what you thought of my story. I'd love to know, what you liked and how the story made you feel. Please feel free to drop me a line at grivante@thezeebrothers.com to share your thoughts. Or, if you have time, I'd love it if you could take a few moments to leave a review on Amazon, Goodreads, Facebook or wherever you as a reader hang out online.

A review doesn't have to be complicated or lengthy. It can be as simple as, I liked it because… and then list a couple of things you enjoyed about the story. That's all! Thanks for coming along on this adventure with me!

-Grivante

P.S. Wondering what happens next? What is it about this mysterious Dr. Nitsau that has the brothers so uptight? What secrets from their past are waiting to be revealed? Who is stalking JJ and why? Will Judas ever get his license? And just where is that crazy dog from anyway?

Learn more in The Zee Brothers Vol.3 Halloween Holocaust, a free preview is just a page turn away!

Check out all of the Zee Brothers Stories on Amazon!

THE ZEE BROTHERS
ZOMBIE EXTERMINATORS
NOVELS

SHORTS & MINI COMICS

WWW.THEZEEBROTHERS.COM

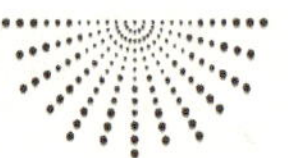
GRIVANTE

THE ZEE BROTHERS

ZOMBIE EXTERMINATORS:
HALLOWEEN HOLOCAUST

BONUS CHAPTER #1 (BURT B' GONE)

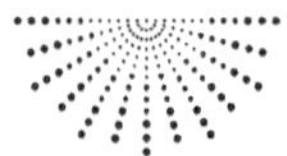

8:03PM

Knock! Knock!

Tom Peterson lowered the volume on his television and smiled at his daughters. The two of them sat side-by-side on the couch, still wearing near-identical Dora the Explorer costumes and comparing their Halloween goodies.

"I'll trade you my chocolate bar for your Sweet-Tarts," Mckenzie said to her younger sibling as their father got up from his seat.

"Nu-uh!" Patricia lifted her bag to the other side of the couch.

Tom picked up his candy dish and opened the door, ready to shut things down after this final batch of trick-or-treaters. On his porch, he didn't find the kids in cute costumes he expected, but two large men in suits. One with a tie, the other with a sports coat and black t-shirt.

"Hello, Sir," the man on the left said and thrust a brochure into Tom's hand. "We're here to talk about Jesus."

Tom scrunched his face and glanced at the pamphlet which

showed Jesus holding his hands out, a pile of candy in them. Tom shook his head.

"Sorry, guys, but we're not interested." He handed the brochure back.

Neither of the men took it. Instead, the man to the right held up a basket containing bright green candy in a style of package Tom hadn't ever seen. "We're reverse trick-or-treating."

"Reverse trick-or-treating? Tom asked, raising his eyebrows.

"Yes," the man answered. "We bring treats to you."

Tom shook his head again. "Look, guys, my daughters got plenty of candy already, plus," he held up the dish in his hand, "we still have all this. Let's just call it a night, shall we?"

The men grinned at each other, shrugged and stepped to the side, creating an opening. Behind them, a tall thin woman, with long, wavy black hair waited. She wore a knee-length white lab coat and until she stepped into the light, Tom thought she looked quite attractive.

"I guess it'll be a trick then," the woman said as she rushed forward, knocking the dish from his hands and tackling him to the floor. "Trick-or-treat, what kind of tasty brains do you have for me to eat?" The woman's face was a Jeckel and Hyde combination; one side smooth and beautiful, the other a disfigured mask of exposed muscle with her right eye clouded over amidst the mangled flesh.

The two young girls on the couch screamed as the woman tore their father's ear from his face.

BURT, yes that Burt, heard a cry outside and got up to look out his front window. A group of teenagers ran along the sidewalk giggling and laughing. He shook his head. "Them were the days." He watched the noisy group disappear down the street.

On his neighbor's porch, stood three adults in costumes. Two guys in suits and... what is that woman wearing, he asked himself? She looks like a slutty Snow White.

From what he could see in the dim light of Mr. & Mrs. Simmon's house, she wore heels, nylons and a long white coat that came to a stop just above her knees.

"A bit old for trick-or-treating," Burt muttered. "Teenagers."

His eyes drifted to the street where at the corner a van sat parked. Its dark boxy shape made it stand out as it wasn't a vehicle normally parked there. He moved on, lots of parents followed their kids around in cars these days.

Movement from his neighbor's porch grabbed his attention, he no longer saw the woman and the two men were entering the house.

"Oh," Burt grimaced as he turned away. Even worse than teenage trick-or-treaters, missionaries.

He heard a faint cry, more a shriek really, followed by voices yelling and made his way to the slider at the back of the house. It opened into a small backyard, fenced along the back with waist-high chain link. Behind that, stood an open field that all the houses surrounded. It included a shared pagoda for family picnics and a kid's playground that remained perpetually under construction. More than one house hustled and bustled with lights, music, and adults partying in their costumes, but no one seemed to be screaming, at least not any longer. Halloween. You couldn't trust your eyes or your ears, it was just as bad as April Fool's Day.

He cracked the door open, listening for a minute to the thump of music, faint voices, and laughter from the partiers, nothing out of the ordinary. He stepped back and looked at his reflection in the glass. Dark circles ringed the eyes on his gaunt face. He let out a sigh, how many Halloweens or even holidays did he have left to enjoy, he wondered? He shook his head and walked away from the slider, leaving it open a few inches.

He wandered back to the front and glanced outside, seeing a few groups of bigger kids walking door to door on the opposite side of the street. Most houses were going dark for the night, including his next-door neighbors, he noticed. Wonder where the two men and slutty Snow White had gone, he shrugged. As long as they don't come knocking here.

By the front door lay a mostly empty bowl of candy. He shut off the porch light and clicked the lock. "That's enough for this year."

He wheezed as he walked back to his stained and ripped recliner. Beside the chair, sat a small side table with a lamp, its shade lopsided. A large laptop computer and a dozen pill bottles sat near the lamp. With the pills was a bright blue bag of Burt's favorite, Mighty Menthol Cough Drops. He reached in and grabbed one before plopping into his chair. He unwrapped it and tossed the wrapper over his shoulder to join the dozens already behind the recliner before placing his computer on his lap.

"Now where was I?"

Paused on the screen before him was an animated movie involving tentacles and a naked woman. He clicked play.

"No! Stop!" The woman cried out as the purple tentacles slithered across her flesh encircling her. The suction cups grasped at her skin, pulling her arms and legs away from her body, yet the creature itself remained unseen.

Knock! Knock!

Knuckles rapped on his front door and Burt jumped in his seat. He smacked the pause button and glared. "Damn kids. The light's off," he muttered, waited a moment and then hit play again. "They'll go away."

The woman on the screen fought the beast, tugging her arms away, trying to break free. The tentacled monster yanked each of her limbs, pulling them taut until it had her spread-eagled. One lone tentacle roamed her naked flesh, making its way down her chest, over her navel and —

Knock! Knock!

Burt hit pause again and clenched on the cough drop, crushing it to pieces in his mouth. "Dagnammit!" He tossed the laptop onto the side table, knocking the pill bottles over and scattering them like bowling pins. He slammed the footrest down and then pushed himself up with both arms.

At the door, he grumbled about greedy children, but picked up the candy bowl and flipped on the light. He undid the lock before gazing through the peephole to decide how grumpy to be.

Only it wasn't kids. It was two rather large men in dark suits. Who the hell are they supposed to be? Secret Service? Agents of Shield? Behind them he could make out the vague shape of the woman he'd seen earlier from the side, her face was— "Whoa!" he said aloud. "That's some impressive makeup."

Red dripped from the woman's face like a still wet mask painted on. Her right eye clouded in a sunken and mottled cheek. Blackish-red lines running down her neck and over the heft of her breast.

Burt's eyes stopped at her cleavage. "What's her costume... A slutty zombie princess?"

Then she spoke, muffled though it was through the door. "We don't have all night. Don't bother with the candy this time, just push in when it opens." The woman's cloudy eye stared straight ahead, her mouth gnashing up and down in a chewing motion.

"What the fuck?" Burt's hand fell away from the door handle, his heart racing. He set the bowl on the table next to it and peered back out the peephole.

"Try the handle," the grisly woman spoke.

Burt's stomach dropped and his hand shot out, grabbing the knob as it turned.

"Oh crap!" He slammed his small body against the door, grasping for the lock as the handle twisted in his grip. He clicked it over, and the knob shook but didn't turn. He stared ahead, panting.

"It's locked," the man said.

"Fine," the woman said. "Let's get to the next one. It's time the real party got started around here."

Burt watched, heart pounding in his chest as the trio stepped away from his porch, walked down the sidewalk and went to the neighbor's house on the other side of him. He crept over to his side window, peering out.

These neighbors were an older retired couple who loved the holiday and it showed. Giant spiders clung to the outside of their home, inflatable ghouls and ghosts lined the yard, bobbing back and forth. When the men knocked on the door, it opened a moment later.

Burt continued watching through the window which looked directly into his neighbor's house. The couple stood together, in their own costumes, Minnie and Mickey Mouse, holding a large bowl of full-size candy bars. "Trick-or-treat!" they yelled with big welcoming grins.

The men stepped aside and Burt could hear the woman on the porch speaking, "It's a trick for you, but a treat for me." She rushed into the room, knocking the old lady to the floor sending the bowl of candy flying into the air; pieces shot everywhere like a grenade exploding.

There were shouts and cries from his neighbor Bob, but the men stepped into the house and grabbed him, holding him in place while his wife screamed.

Burt's mouth hung open. He couldn't see everything, but he saw enough. He backed away from the window, reaching into his back pocket and pulling out his wallet. With shaking fingers, he fumbled through the cards lodged there until he found the one he needed.

Zee Brothers: Zombie Exterminators
Jonah & Judas : Owner Operators
888-867-5309
Ask for Jenny
"We keep the dead, dead!"

BONUS CHAPTER #2 (THE ZEE BROTHERS)

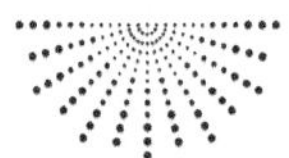

Bzzzz!

The Zee Brother's phone lay in the kitchen vibrating quietly. Jonah and Judas sat side by side on the couch mashing buttons on their game controllers. Half drunk beers lay on the table before them next to a smoldering joint in an ashtray.

"Get him, Judas!" Jonah shouted.

"I'm trying, bro! There's too damn many and I can't find where the ammo drop is. I'm out!"

Jonah's head bobbed and weaved, responding to the action on the screen. "C'mon!" He slammed buttons on his controller, grimaced and set it down, exchanging it for his beer. "I'm out unless you can come revive me."

Judas jammed the stick on his controller, his body twisting, beads of sweat running from underneath the brim of his backward hat. "C'mon," he grit his teeth, exhaling a loud sigh. "Damn!"

On the screen, a horde of undead monsters tackled his character before fading to black. Blood-red letters appeared dripping the words, 'You Died!'.

Judas picked up his own beer. "That was a good one. I don't think we've made it that far before. We only had a hundred and seven miles to go to Lakota! I thought for sure we'd make it back to the Peterbilt."

"We would've made it further if that damn boss hadn't spawned right behind me. I wasn't ready for him."

"No, me either. I—"

Knock! Knock!

They glanced at each other.

"Did you order another pizza?" Jonah asked, raising an eyebrow.

"No. Though I could totally eat another one," Judas laughed.

Jonah chuckled. "Me too. Go answer it and I'll grab the phone and order one up. Pepperoni, jalapeños and extra sauce?"

"Can we get double jalapeños?"

Jonah downed the rest of his beer and headed for the kitchen. "Abso-lutely!"

"I hope it's not more trick-or-treaters. We shoulda closed the gate when we got home."

"Then how would the pizza guy get in?"

"Hmm, good point." Judas stood up and dusted crumbs off his shirt before walking to the main door of their converted garage.

Jonah glanced at the screen on his phone.

'5 New Voicemails'

He shook his head and muttered under his breath. "Frickin Halloween pranksters."

At the door, Judas paused a moment, the thought of a spicy pizza making his mouth water, which always kicked in his cravings for nicotine. He grabbed a mint out of his pocket and swung the door open.

What he saw there made him cry out and stumble back, tripping over Pots, their grey, and white cat.

"Ahh!"

He slammed into the floor as the cat took off, disappearing behind the couch.

Jonah tossed his phone down mid-dial and came running. "What is it, bro?"

He stopped short when he found Judas, pale-faced and scurrying away from the open door like a backward crab.

Jonah's eyes swept up the entry. Wearing red sneakers, white bobby socks, a short black, and red cheerleading skirt and a matching skin-tight half-top with the letters ZX monogrammed across the front, stood a gore-covered, zombie-eyed JJ.

"Wh-what?" Judas panted from the floor.

Jonah's hand reached for the usually present form of Brutus but swished through empty space just as JJ started laughing and apologizing.

She stepped inside and squatted in front of Judas, reaching out a hand. "I'm sorry, sugar. I didn't mean to scare you. It's only make-up!" She looked him in the eyes and gave her best, 'you can't be mad at someone this cute' smile. With the professionally done zombie make-up, it didn't work.

Pots reappeared from behind the couch and ran over to twirl himself around JJ's leg. Pans lay on the back of the couch watching the scene with typical feline indifference.

"JJ," Judas shook his head, "you scared me half to death."

Her face softened and she took his hand. "Sorry, Judas. A cosmetic artist friend of mine did it for me and I came by to see if you two would like to go to a Halloween party with me? I even have a costume for Larry." She grinned and raised her eye's at him. "We're gonna be Craig and Arianna, the cheerleading duo from Saturday Night Live!"

"No!" Jonah boomed from beside them, causing JJ to cringe and Pots to scurry away again. "We told you before," Jonah said, "we don't do Halloween."

JJ took Judas's hand and helped them both to stand. She turned to Jonah looking at his scruffy unshaven face and frowning. "What, are you two to macho to dress up?"

Xanadu trotted in from behind her, a pair of black and red pom-pom's in his mouth. He set them at her feet.

"No," Jonah said, his tone softening.

JJ bent over and grabbed the pom-poms. "C'mon. It'll be fun. You can dress up as Hans and Franz! It'll be great." She shot her right arm above her head, shaking them. "Let's go Zee Brothers!"

Judas laughed and Jonah bit his tongue, struggling not to grin.

JJ brought the pom-pom to her chest, then threw both hands up in a Y. "Yay! Zombie Exterminators! Fight, fight, win!" She spun around, sending the skirt flying up and revealing the number sixty-nine on the back of her uniform.

"Oh my," Judas said, taking in the skimpy cheerleading outfit.

She smiled at him, leaned in and kissed his cheek, before growling like a zombie in his ear. "C'mon, let's go have some fun!"

"No!" Jonah said again, less forceful, but still resolute.

She studied him. "What's the matter? Why are you such a party-pooper?"

Jonah sighed and scratched the back of his neck. "For two reasons. One, Judas has his driver's test at 8am and two, we don't do Halloween for exactly this reason!" He waved his hand in her direction.

"You don't like women in skimpy outfits?" She cocked her head to the right and raised an eyebrow at him.

"No," Jonah shook his head, resigned. "It's the make-up."

Judas's cheeks flared red and he turned away.

Jonah continued. "We can't tell the real dead from those pretending to be. When we were still new to zombie exterminating, we got a call on Halloween. We went out, some jackass decided to play a prank on us. Judas shot him."

"Oh!" JJ's mouth fell open, color draining from her face.

"We kept telling him we were going to shoot and he kept

pretending. Luckily, Judas's first shot only hit him in the arm and then he was on the ground crying like a baby, but it could've been worse."

"I'm so sorry," JJ said. "I had no idea. I should've thought through my costume a little better."

"I kinda dig it," Judas blurted, then added, "From the neck down anyway."

JJ gave him a giggling growl.

Jonah's phone vibrated on the counter, causing JJ to glance between it and Jonah. "Aren't you going to answer that?"

"Nope." Jonah shook his head. "It's nothing but pranksters all night long. April Fool's Day and Halloween. Everyone thinks they're a comedian."

"Well, what do you do?"

"We take the night off." He waved his hands at the table in the living room, littered with beer cans and the empty Big Daddy's pizza box.

She looked at the television screen where the title of the game flashed. 'Zombie Road: The Game!' "That doesn't look like a night off," she chuckled.

The brothers both laughed.

"Well, darn it." She put the pom-poms under her arm and pulled a rubber ring with a large red ball on it off her wrist. "I even had props for Larry."

"What is that," Judas asked.

"It's a ball gag. I know he doesn't have any teeth, but I figure it'll keep him from being a nuisance."

"What did you say you wanted to dress him up as?" Jonah asked.

"You've seen Saturday Night Live right?"

Both brothers nodded.

"Remember the cheerleaders played by Will Farrell & Cheri Oteri?"

The brothers nodded again, grins breaking across their faces.

"Well, we're them, but zombies cheering on you two!"

Jonah and Judas broke into laughter, shaking their heads.

"That's ridiculous!" Judas said smiling.

"Right?" JJ beamed back. "Anyway, guess it's out of the question. Mind if I hang out with you two instead?"

"Sure!" Judas blurted and rushed to grab a large orange package off the kitchen table.

Pots joined Pans on the back of the couch to watch the trio. JJ caught sight of them and hurried over. "Well hello you two! How's my favorite rodent killers doing?" She scratched their heads and turned back to the brothers. "I'll even take this make-up off, makes my face itch anyway."

Xanadu trotted over, hopped on the couch and looked at the cats with a sigh before curling into a ball. Here's good.

Judas returned carrying the orange box and holding it out to JJ. "I uh, got you these." He smiled, shifting on his feet. "Happy Halloween." Behind him, Jonah looked away.

Eyebrows raised, she took the box from him. "Well, what's this? I love presents" She popped the lid open and grinned at what she found. "A giant peanut butter cup shaped like a pumpkin? Yay! You sure know how to be sweet! Thank you!" She set it on the table and kissed his cheek. "Let me get this make-up off and then we'll dig in!"

A few minutes later, the trio huddled on the couch, controllers in hand, the message, 'You Died!' displayed again.

"I don't get it," JJ said, "they're much easier to kill in real life. Why are these so fast? Do those really exist?"

"Only in Hollywood," Jonah answered.

"Hmph," JJ set the controller down. "That's no fun." She picked up a chunk of the giant candy and took a bite. In the kitchen, the phone vibrated again, getting her attention. "Can I listen to them?"

"What, why?" Jonah asked.

"It's gotta be funner than sitting here dying every two minutes."

"Fine," Jonah shrugged.

JJ got up and bounced happily to the kitchen, both brothers turning to watch her go. They looked at each other.

"Damn, I love her," Judas sighed.

Jonah scoffed, "Yeah, she's infuriatingly adorkable."

They resumed playing without JJ, until a moment later when she shouted at them from the kitchen.

"Hey!"

Jonah hit pause and turned to see JJ holding his phone, the expression on her face making his heart race. Tight lips, gritted teeth, narrow eyes and reddening cheeks, she was about to blow, her eyes flicked up and bored into them.

"Have you boys been taking pictures of me when I wasn't looking?"

"Huh?" Jonah scrunched his face. "What are you talking about?"

"Mhm, no idea, huh?" She walked over, sat down in-between them and shoved the phone in Jonah's face. On the screen, there was a picture of JJ's round butt in tight blue jeans as she was bent over scratching Xanadu behind the ears. "Then what's this? This is from the dog park the other day!"

Jonah stammered. "I-I didn't take that."

Both he and JJ swiveled to look at Judas who had slid to the far end of the couch, cheeks bright as apples.

"So it was you, huh?"

"Y-yes."

JJ frowned and looked back at the phone, flipping through the photos.

"Hmm."

Swipe.

"That one's kinda hot."

Swipe.

"Nice angle."

Swipe.

"Ohh," she grinned as a rather cute shot of her appeared. "Maybe you should've been a photographer."

Swipe.

"No!" She shook her head at a blurry unfocused shot that had her looking like a mutated potato. "Not this one."

Delete. Swipe.

"No." Her tone getting gruffer as she swiped and deleted a few in a row. "No. No." She muttered under her breath. "You can't take bad photos of me."

"Ok, ok," Judas agreed, nodding. "I won't take any more photos of you."

Her head snapped to look at him, hair swinging out and smacking Jonah in the face beside her. "No. I didn't say that! I just don't want to know about it and if there are pictures, they better not be bad ones!"

Judas swallowed and touched the base of his neck. "So, um, what?" He leaned forward. "Only take good photos?"

JJ nodded and smiled. "And try to catch me by surprise. Delete any that aren't flattering."

"Ok," Judas smiled back. "I can do that."

"Good," she said, standing and heading to the bathroom, phone still in her hand.

The brothers watched the door close with matching looks of confusion.

"Why'd she take the phone with her?" Judas asked.

Jonah shrugged. "No idea."

"Women are confusing. She told us what she wants, but it could be completely different tomorrow. How are we supposed to keep up?"

Jonah opened his mouth to reply when the bathroom door swung back open.

JJ beamed, clicking away on the phone as she rejoined them on the couch with a devilish grin.

"Let's listen to these prank calls!"

※

FIND out what happens next in The Zee Brothers: Halloween Holocaust on Amazon!

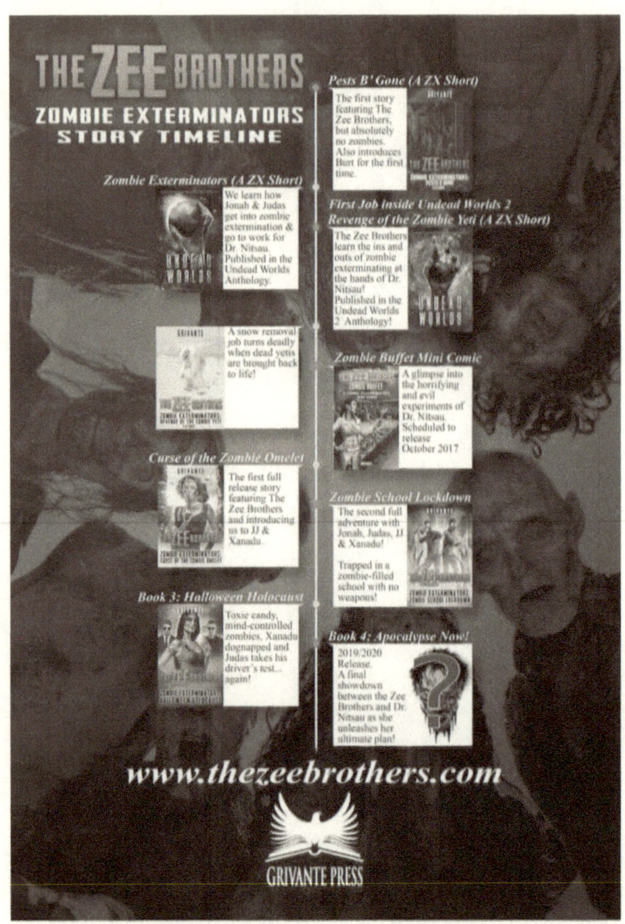
THE ZEE BROTHERS
ZOMBIE EXTERMINATORS
STORY TIMELINE

Zombie Exterminators (A ZX Short)
We learn how Jonah & Judas get into zombie extermination & go to work for Dr. Nitsau. Published in the Undead Worlds Anthology.

A snow removal job turns deadly when dead yetis are brought back to life!

Curse of the Zombie Omelet
The first full release story featuring The Zee Brothers and introducing us to JJ & Xanadu.

Book 3: Halloween Holocaust
Toxic candy, mind-controlled zombies, Xanadu dognapped and Judas takes his driver's test... again!

Pests B' Gone (A ZX Short)
The first story featuring The Zee Brothers, but absolutely no zombies. Also introduces Burt for the first time.

First Job inside Undead Worlds 2
Revenge of the Zombie Yeti (A ZX Short)
The Zee Brothers learn the ins and outs of zombie exterminating at the hands of Dr. Nitsau! Published in the Undead Worlds 2 Anthology!

Zombie Buffet Mini Comic
A glimpse into the horrifying and evil experiments of Dr. Nitsau. Scheduled to release October 2017

Zombie School Lockdown
The second full adventure with Jonah, Judas, JJ & Xanadu!
Trapped in a zombie-filled school with no weapons!

Book 4: Apocalypse Now!
2019/2020 Release. A final showdown between the Zee Brothers and Dr. Nitsau as she unleashes her ultimate plan!

www.thezeebrothers.com

GRIVANTE PRESS

ABOUT THE AUTHOR

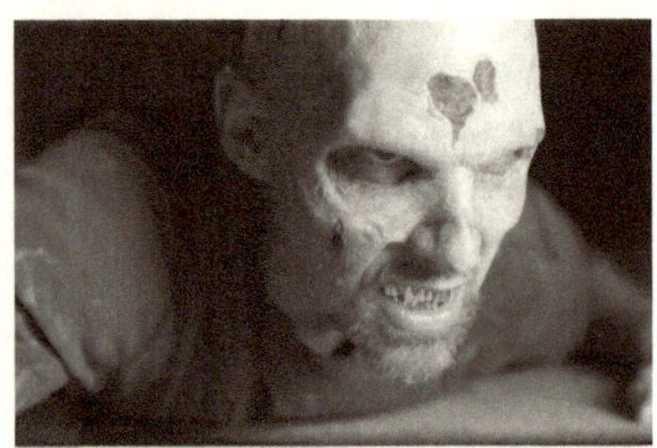

Grivante, pronounced "Gri-von-tay", enjoys writing humorous and bizarre fiction. He hopes you laugh as much reading his works as he does writing them. He's hard at work on the final book in The Zee Brothers series, either that or he's doing something completely unproductive. Yeah… he's probably doing that one. Well, when he does get it finished, it'll be called, 'Zombie Apocalypse Now!" Be on the look out for it in 2019/2020. Visit www.grivantepress.com or the social media links below to find more by this author!

BB bookbub.com/authors/grivante

facebook.com/grivante

twitter.com/grivante

instagram.com/grivante

WANT MORE ZOMBIES?

Visit http://www.grivantepress.com/reanimatedwriters/

9 781626 760172